SOPHIE AND *SCOTTIE'S*
Adventures *of the*
Monarch Mystery

Cindy C. Murray

Sophie and Scottie's Adventures
of the Monarch Mystery

Published by Madmac Press

For inquires contact:
Madmac Press
1-858-337-1102
Rowlett, TX 75088

Printed in the United States of America

ISBN-13: 978-1-7323134-0-8

Library of Congress Control Number 2014939773

Cover art by Molly Alice Hoy
Book design by Drew Bailey

To my loving family and their support of my adventurous hopes and dreams for this book and all of the books to come.

Table
of
Contents

Introduction

The 10,000-acre ranch was a great place for Sophie and Scottie—or Scarlet as Ma liked to call her to get Scottie's attention—to grow up. The rolling hills to run down, cool ponds to swim in, huge oak trees to climb, and miles of trails to ride their horses made it paradise for the girls.

Their home, called Shear Heaven Ranch, consisted of a dorm for the ranch hands, a main ranch house with its red tile roof and adobe brick walls, a large barn, and lots of horse corrals and grazing fields for the sheep. It was perfect for raising sheep, cattle, horses, dogs, and cats. The rats and raccoons came on their own.

The key business on the ranch was selling wool. This required lots and lots and lots—you get the idea—of sheep. Scottie and Sophie's Ma and Pa, who loved fuzzy white-faced sheep (to the girls' delight), were sheep-shearing and wool-selling ranchers before the girls were even born.

The girls loved the ruggedness as well as the beauty of the ranch. They couldn't help but admire the wild flowers that were in full bloom. Sophie and Scottie would follow the butterflies floating from plant to plant, hoping one would land on them if they kept really still.

"Boy, am I glad school is out!" Scottie exclaimed as she tried to catch a butterfly.

"Me too," Sophie agreed while running next to Scottie. "I hope this summer will be fun and exciting. I'm not sure it will be, though, way out here on the ranch."

"Oh, it will be a great summer. We get to take care of Fuzzy Mama, ride our horses, and who knows . . . I feel like something is going to happen to us."

"Like what?" Sophie asked while picking some wild flowers for Ma.

"I'm not sure. It's a mystery to me," Scottie replied in a rather thoughtful manner. "I think all we can do is to keep our eyes open to things on the ranch that don't seem, well, normal."

"Okay, if you say so," Sophie said as she realized it was lunch time and then reached over to tap Scottie on the shoulder. "Last one home is a rotten egg!" Sophie shouted and sprinted across the field toward the ranch house.

CHAPTER ONE

Shear Heaven

Scottie slid the large weathered barn door open to the left just enough to step into the middle aisle-way of the massive room. Her worn tan leather cowboy boots clicked on the wood floor of the barn as she made her way down to the other end. Scottie loved being in the barn, and as she got closer to the other end, she could hear rustling of straw in the large pen.

"Good morning, Fuzzy Mama," Scottie said as she filled the large round-bellied ewe's feed bucket full of green alfalfa straw pellets. Scottie and Sophie were in charge of keeping watch on Fuzzy Mama because she was going to have a baby any day now.

"Scarlet, where are you?"

"You call me Scarlet one more time and I'm going to

shovel this dirty straw all over you!" Scottie answered back in an irritated voice.

"Boy, are you grumpy," Sophie said as she walked down to the sheep's pen. "Any signs of the baby yet?"

"Not yet," Scottie replied as she scooped up more soiled straw from the pen. "Well, don't just stand there. Get another shovel or that rake over there and help me clean Fuzzy Mama's pen."

"Okay, okay, don't be so bossy! Just because you got to the barn before me doesn't mean you get to tell me what to do."

Both girls went to work cleaning out Fuzzy Mama's birthing pen. Scottie and Sophie earned this responsible chore because they were now 11 years old.

"And a half!" the girls would chime in to correct Ma or Pa when their age would come up in a conversation. Both were tall for their age and quite athletic. Sophie loved to jazz dance and Scottie took tap. Both girls loved to play soccer and horseback ride.

"I could ride Starburst all day and compete in barrel racing and all the roping events 'till the cows come home," Scottie would say to Pa after each horse show. Sophie competed in horse shows, too, but mostly in a slower paced class called Western Pleasure.

Starburst, Scottie's shiny dark brown horse with flowing black mane and tail, had a white star between her eyes and one white "sock" on her front left leg.

Sophie loved to tease Scottie about Starburst and say, "You should call Starburst Peg Leg because she looks like her leg is in a white cast all the time."

"Very funny!" Scottie would reply close to Sophie's face. "But looks aren't everything!"

And then both girls would laugh and race their horses to the other end of the horse arena.

Sophie's horse, Firefly, was a beautiful chestnut reddish-brown with a deep red mane and tail. Firefly looked like flames were blowing in the wind from her tail when she'd gallop or run. Both horses loved to compete with each other, and the sisters never seemed to get tired of it either.

Even Pa would notice that the girls' high energy and their ability to try new things seemed never ending. Heck, Pa thought to himself, if I could bottle their energy, I'd make millions!

Each girl had the same small nose and shaped mouth and chin, but they weren't identical. Sophie had green eyes with long straight dark brown hair with red highlights, as Sophie would describe it to her Ma while brushing it at night.

Scottie, on the other hand, had blue eyes with long wavy red hair and blond streaks through it.

"It's the kiss of the sun that lightens my hair," Scottie would say in a high-and-mighty voice to Sophie.

And, of course, Sophie would reply, "That's no kiss. Your hair is streaked from all of the dirt you get in it all the time!"

Even with all of their teasing, Scottie and Sophie seemed to make a pretty good team on the ranch.

"Hey, do you hear that?" Sophie asked with the rake in her hand. "I think Ma is ringing the bell. Yep, breakfast is ready." She quickly threw down the rake, jumped over the pen's low railing, and shouted, "Last one home is a rotten egg!"

Scottie jumped over the rail too, shouting over her shoulder, "We'll be back Fuzzy Mama." She then ran out of the barn after Sophie.

"Hi, Sophie," Ma greeted her as she put a platter full of steaming blueberry pancakes on the table next to a bowl of scrambled eggs and a plate of crispy bacon. "Has Fuzzy Mama had her baby yet?"

"No, not yet," Sophie answered as she sat down on the large oak bench next to the kitchen table. "I can't believe that this is her fifth lamb."

"And they're so cute when they're first born," Scottie said breathlessly when she pushed open the screen door of the kitchen doorway and sat down next to Sophie.

"Hi, Pa!" The girls greeted him at the same time as he walked through the doorway.

"Who left the barn door open?" Pa asked in an irritated sounding voice.

"I guess I did," Scottie answered.

"You need to be more careful when you leave the barn," Pa scolded while looking at both girls. "It would be a shame to put Fuzzy Mama in harm's way since she's big and slow with that big belly of hers. That lamb is due any minute and a coyote would love to have her as a main dish and her baby as dessert."

"Oh, Pa, do you have to be so gruesome?" Sophie complained.

"You're right, Pa. We'll, I mean, I will be more careful next time I close the door," Scottie replied.

As the family ate breakfast, Pa looked out the win-

14

dow and saw postal worker Wilson walking up the dirt driveway toward the front door.

"Can you girls go see what Mr. Wilson is delivering?" Pa asked. Both girls were away from the table and running toward the large double mahogany wood doors in the entrance hall before he rang the doorbell.

"Good morning, girls," Mr. Wilson said in a cheery voice. "Here's your regular mail and a package addressed to Miss Sophie and Miss Scottie Pratt."

The girls looked at each other with wide eyes and took the mail and package from him.

"Good morning, Jed," Ma greeted as she was walking down the hall toward the front doors to see what was taking the girls so long.

"Good morning, Kathryn," Jed replied. "I usually wouldn't come up the driveway off the main road, but I thought the girls would like to see this 'special delivery' as soon as possible."

"That was very thoughtful of you. Would you like some coffee?" Ma asked.

"No thanks. I've got to keep going and make all my deliveries. Maybe next time. Oh, by the way, I heard a commotion in your barn while I was walking toward your front door." Right after Mr. Wilson said that, the girls heard a loud tweet, tweet whistle sound.

"Fuzzy Mama!" the girls yelled at the same time.

Scottie quickly shoved the mail and package into Ma's arms and followed Sophie as they ran down the dirt driveway toward the barn. They could hear lots of bleating from the ewe as they ran into the barn. The door was already open. When the girls reached the birthing pen, there sat Pa on the fence railing, watching Fuzzy Mama to see if she needed any help.

"Glad you two heard my whistle."

The girls hopped into the pen and were ready to help Pa with Fuzzy Mama if asked. Seconds later Pa pointed to Fuzzy's backside and there you could see the baby lamb's nose and two front hooves. Very quickly the entire lamb was born. Sophie and Scottie looked at each other, smiled, and stood up to hug Pa. The baby nuzzled Fuzzy Mama and tried to stand up so it could begin to suckle for its first meal.

"Pa, how did you know the baby was coming now?" Scottie asked.

"I stood up to go outside and say hello to Jed and noticed Jack down toward the barn waving his arms back and forth. So I figured Fuzzy Mama was havin' her baby and I'd better run down to see if she was. Sure enough, Fuzzy was ready, so I whistled to get you girls down here to the barn," Pa answered.

"It's so cute and cuddly. Look at that snowy white face and tiny black nose," Sophie observed.

"Come on, Scottie, let's get the small pitchforks and take out the soiled straw and put down fresh straw for the new family," Sophie said with a smile.

For most of the day, Scottie and Sophie hung out in the barn. They took a break with a picnic lunch Ma packed for them. They ate it at a large oak table with benches next to the barn. When they finished, the girls put halters on their horses and, by using a rope that clipped onto the halter, they led their horses back to the barn to brush them until their coats were shiny.

Sophie decided to braid Firefly's beautiful long mane.

"This summer is turning out to be great," Scottie said with enthusiasm. "The horses are so fun to ride and take care of, and Fuzzy Mama now has her own healthy baby to take care of, too."

"And," Sophie continued, "this lamb won't get out of the pasture and get lost like her last one did."

"It definitely won't," Pa said while walking up to the girls as they kept grooming the horses. "There's not much more we can do for Fuzzy Mama now. Be sure she has plenty of alfalfa pellets and water after you put the horses back in their corrals. Then head on up to the house and wash up for dinner."

"Okay, Pa," the girls said at the same time, as twins often do.

After the girls finished putting the horses back in their corral and feeding Fuzzy Mama, Scottie turned to Sophie and said, "This time you're going to be the rotten egg!"

Both girls quickly hopped over the railing and ran toward the barn door. Scottie was just ahead of Sophie as they headed for the house.

"Don't forget to close the door, Sophie!" Scottie shouted over her shoulder as she kept running toward the ranch house.

"Whoa, whoa girls," Ma said. "You're going to break the door, storming in that way."

"Sorry, Ma," Scottie replied as Sophie came charging in after her through the kitchen doorway.

"We're going to wash up and change into clean clothes," Sophie huffed while both girls stood bent over, hands on their knees as they caught their breath.

"Honestly, girls, you'd think you were running in the Olympics the way you both sprinted in here!" Ma said in an amused but stern voice. "So how are Fuzzy and the baby?"

"They're perfect," the girls exclaimed at the same time.

"Oh, Ma," Scottie began, "where did you put the package that Mr. Wilson delivered?"

"Oh, yeah," Sophie remembered, "with all the commotion about Fuzzy Mama, I totally forgot about the package."

"I put it on the table in your room," Ma answered. "It looks like Auntie Jill sent it during one of her many travels. I remember when she went to some remote Indian reservation and she got you girls the oddest boxes."

"No, Ma," Sophie added. "They're not odd boxes. They're rain boxes. It says on the explanation sheets that came with the boxes. Mine is red leather with a beautiful beaded pattern on the lid, and Scottie's is midnight blue leather with beads on the leather too."

"I think Ma's right," Scottie agreed. "They are kind of weird. I mean, when you open the lid, instead of music, you hear a kind of chanting with a drumbeat in the background. I still can't figure out how it works. The info sheet just says to shake the box for a few seconds and open the lid. I don't know if the boxes can really make it rain, but it's neat to think that it does work."

"Enough talk about boxes and beads. Go get washed up for dinner. It will be ready in one hour," ordered Ma with a smile.

The girls hurried out of the kitchen, past the front entrance hall, and toward their room.

18

CHAPTER TWO

Open it!
Open it!

As the girls walked into their room, Scottie went over to the large wood table that was just in front of the bedroom door. She picked up the rectangular package and read the return address. Ma was right. The gift was from Auntie Jill and it was about the size of a shoe box.

"Well, are you going to stare at it or open it?" Sophie asked in a sarcastic tone.

Scottie walked over to her side of the room and sat down on her bed. Their room was like a long rectangle, with each girl claiming one side. The bunk beds that were used by the ranch hands were removed long ago. The girls now had lots of space for beds, desks, a bathroom, and two walk-in closets.

The center table just inside their room was about a

5-foot-round oak table and was considered the "safe zone." This meant that an item could be set on it and either girl could look at it, use it, or play with the item without being yelled at by the other.

Scottie and Sophie could tell that this package was special. Heck, Auntie Jill rarely sent anything unless it was, let's say, unusual. Scottie carefully took off the brown shipping paper that covered the package and an envelope dropped onto her lap.

"Ooh, a card," Sophie squealed. "We should probably read it before we open the rest of the package. Look at the wrapping paper. It's so brightly colored, like one of those really pretty blankets from South America or Mexico."

"Since you get to unwrap the gift, I'm taking this," Sophie continued as she quickly took the card from Scottie's lap.

Dear Sophie and Scottie,

I'm giving this special gift to you both because you've proven to me how mature you two can be. When your father told me he put you in charge of Fuzzy Mama's birthing pen, I first thought this was too much responsibility. But when he told me about last spring's lamb dilemma and how you solved it, I knew you two were ready for this gift and the responsibilities that come with it. This gift will show you many places and you will meet special and nice people. Enjoy your gift, and use it wisely.

Love, Auntie Jill

"Wow," Sophie said as she looked up at Scottie, "I didn't know Pa told Auntie Jill about Fuzzy Mama's lamb, uh, adventure. Gosh, I remember it like it was yesterday," Sophie thought out loud remembering—

Sophie and Scottie were riding on the Oak Branch trail on the ranch during their school's spring break. Suddenly, Scottie heard something.

"Did you hear that?" Scottie asked Sophie. "I think it's coming from over there." She pointed to an area away from the trail behind some rocks and bushes. Scottie steered Starburst over toward the sound.

"Stop, Scottie! It's too dangerous!" Sophie yelled. "The sun is setting and it will be dark soon."

"Oh, stop fussing. I'll get off Starburst and you hold her reigns while I take a look. I just heard it again! Oh, my gosh, I think it's a lamb bleating. It might be Fuzzy Mama's lamb that we just put out to pasture with her."

Scottie now started to run to that area. "It's so steep that I can't hike down this ravine," Scottie shouted to Sophie. Darn, Scottie thought, I wish I could jump super far so I could get down there. Suddenly, Scottie saw some movement on the other side of the rocky ravine. Both girls could hear the cries this time. Sure enough, it was Fuzzy Mama's baby.

"Sophie," Scottie yelled, "tie up the horses and come over here. Fuzzy's lamb must've wandered off from the pasture without the sheep dogs seeing it."

When Sophie walked up, she could barely see the lamb within the shadowy rocks. "The lamb must've lost its footing and slid down the side of the ravine. It's so dark. I wish I could see better. The sun is down behind the ridge so we'd better ride back and get some help from Pa when it's daylight. If we try to hike down there now, we'll get into lots of trouble for putting ourselves in danger, too."

"I guess you're right," Scottie agreed. "Let's hope the coyotes feel the same way as we do."

The next morning as the sun began to rise, Scottie, Sophie, and Pa drove the old truck on the Oak Branch trail to where the girls had spotted the trapped lamb. At first, they couldn't find it.

"There it is," Pa pointed out. "Well, I'll be. Look girls, the lamb had the brains to back itself between two large boulders just wide enough to act as protection from the coyotes!"

The lamb perked up when it heard the voices and started to bleat loudly.

"Now," Pa began, "we've got to figure out a way to coax the lamb out of that crevice."

"I know," Sophie started. "Let's go get Fuzzy Mama and then she can encourage the lamb to come out."

Pa and Scottie were skeptical but thought, why not? Fuzzy Mama would soon be missing her baby and could be very helpful in getting the lamb to come to her. So while Pa went back to the sheep pasture to get her, the girls carefully hiked down into the rocky ravine to keep the lamb company and make sure the coyotes didn't try to attack it.

"I don't know," Scottie thought out loud. "Fuzzy is too big to walk down into the ravine so I'm not sure we can get the lamb to come out of its hiding place."

"Well, we'll have to walk Fuzzy up on the edge of the ravine where the lamb can see her. Then we have to hope it will start bleating, which will make

Fuzzy do the same. The lamb will then hear her and run out of the crevice toward her," Sophie replied convincingly with a smile.

"And then," Scottie blurted out, "as the lamb pokes its head out of the crevice, I'll throw the loop of a rope around its cute little head."

"What rope?" Sophie asked.

"The rope I'll get from Pa's truck. He always keeps one in there. I've been practicing back at the ranch, you know, lassoing rocks and bushes and any other thing that will hold still. I'm sure if I really concentrate, I can do it!"

Before Sophie could reply to Scottie's plan, Pa drove up in the truck with Fuzzy Mama tied to the inside of the truck bed. Fuzzy started to bleat loudly, mostly because she was nervous. As Pa untied her, Fuzzy quickly jumped off the truck and landed on the rocky trail. Pa barely caught the rope as she started to run away, not sure where she was going.

"Hold on, Mama," Pa said. "Let me get the other rope from the truck in case we need it and we'll get to work."

"Pa, I have an idea," Scottie yelled. "Throw me the rope you keep in your truck and I'll see if I can lasso the lamb as it sticks its head out of the crevice looking for Fuzzy Mama."

"Okay, we'll see if that works," Pa yelled back. He threw down the rope and the girls started their rescue operation.

Pa walked Fuzzy to the edge of the ravine as Sophie suggested. Sure enough, the lamb bleated and so did

Fuzzy Mama, which made the lamb stick its head out of its protective shelter.

"Scottie!" Sophie shouted. "You weren't ready and didn't even throw the rope."

"I know. I didn't have the rope just right in my hand. I'm ready now," Scottie yelled back.

The lamb backed up into the crevice when he heard Sophie yell at Scottie. Pa and the girls tried again. Fuzzy Mama began to pace back and forth along the edge of the ravine and started to bleat loudly.

This time, Scottie was ready. She raised her arm over her head with the rope securely in her hand, swinging the rope in a circular motion. Round and round, the rope's loop was going over her head. Her other hand was next to her side, clutching the other end of the rope to help her focus. Finally, the lamb stuck his head out as far as its front legs this time.

SWOOSH! The rope looped itself around the lamb's neck so fast that it didn't know what was upon it. Instantly, as the lamb pulled back, the loop tightened around its neck.

Scottie quickly ran up to the lamb while holding the rope and began to pull the lamb out of the crevice.

"Hurry, Sophie!" Scottie yelled as Sophie was cheering. "Help me pull the lamb out before it backs up too much.

"You did it! I didn't think you could, but you did it!" Sophie exclaimed.

Both girls were able to pull the lamb out of the crevice and coax it to walk toward Fuzzy Mama's bleating.

"I'm so proud of you two girls!" Pa shouted. "I knew you could work together."

They both beamed with pride as they rode in the back of the truck with Fuzzy Mama and her now safe baby back to the ranch.

"That was quite a scare," Sophie said as she was thinking back to that spring day. "I'm glad we were able to work together. Now, open Auntie Jill's gift!"

CHAPTER THREE

It's Magical!

Scottie ripped the bright-colored paper off the box in seconds. As the paper fell to the ground, Scottie began to open the box and pull out something wrapped in bright orange tissue paper.

"What is it? What is it?" Sophie asked excitedly.

Scottie unwrapped the tissue paper and held the object in her hand. It was a picture frame, big enough to hold an 8 inch by 10 inch picture.

"Let me see, let me see," ordered Sophie. She took the frame from Scottie's hands and held it in both of hers. "Wow, it's beautiful. It looks like the frame is made out of hundreds of tiny mirrored jewels or crystals."

"Oh, big deal!" Scottie said in a disappointed voice. "I thought she would send us something a little more exciting or weird, like those rain boxes."

"Well, that's not very nice," Sophie replied. "And look," she continued in a higher voice, "the frame seems to change color as you come near it, kind of like those silly mood rings Ma talked about wearing when she was a little girl."

"Yeah, right," Scottie said sarcastically.

"I mean it, Scottie. Look at the color it's changed to since I've been holding it."

The frame changed from a silvery clear color when it was in the box to a deep blue tone, and now in Sophie's hands it was a bright canary yellow.

"I think it's happy next to me," Sophie said with a smile.

"Oh, puleeze," Scottie replied. "I think you're losing it!"

"Okay, then, let's see what color it becomes now," Sophie said in a rather snooty voice as she handed the frame to Scottie.

Scottie held the frame and the crystals immediately changed back to silver and then to a deep, dark ebony. It startled her so much that she dropped the frame, which luckily landed on her bed. Scottie then said in a hesitant voice, "Okay, maybe this frame is different."

"Auntie Jill never sends anything that's ordinary," Sophie observed. "In fact, look at the frame. She's already put a picture in it."

"Well, now, that is weird too," Scottie said as she picked up the frame off of her bed.

This time, Scottie was curious and really looked at the frame more closely. It had what looked like a diamond-shaped piece of glass centered perfectly on the top part of the frame. As she held it, the frame began to change to an ocean blue. Both girls also took a closer look at the photograph in the frame.

"The picture looks like the ranch house," Sophie described. "It has arches in the front and a large three-tiered fountain like ours. But it's next to a road that passes in front of it."

"And it can't be from around here," Scottie observed. "Look at the plants around the house. The area looks like a forest with some tropical plants."

"Wait, I see a small sign on the house at the top of the stairs behind the fountain. It says Rancho de La Joya. I don't think this is a house, Scottie. I think it's a hotel. I guess Auntie Jill took this picture somewhere in Mexico or South America."

"But where is Auntie Jill?" Scottie asked. "Why would she send us a picture of a hotel that looks like our ranch house in a forest without her in it?"

"I don't know," Sophie answered. "Maybe she took the picture because of the similarity to our house and the hotel."

Sophie then picked up the frame and turned it over. "Look, there's a note attached to the back of the frame." Sophie read:

Please do not remove this photograph until I send another one for you to replace it. You will understand why very soon.
Love, Auntie Jill

Sophie looked at Scottie and asked, "Is this gift weird enough for you now?"

"Oh, yes! This is more like our auntie!"

"This frame is so pretty and a little big, so let's put it on the table facing the door. That way everyone can see it as they come into our room," Sophie suggested. "There, it looks great right here." As she set the frame down, it turned a deep red.

"Oh, my gosh!" Scottie blurted out. "We'd better clean up and get ready for dinner. Then we can show Ma and Pa the frame."

Just as the girls stepped into their own closets, Sophie heard something near their bedroom door. She poked her head out of her closet to see what the noise was. Where the table stood, she noticed the frame had moved. In fact, it was now turned around on the side of the table closest to them and it was facing them!

"Scottie, did you move the picture?" Sophie called out.

"No," Scottie replied, "my arms can't reach that far!"

How weird, Sophie thought as she walked back into her closet to put on some clean clothes. As she walked out, she noticed that the picture was now on the wood floor in front of the table.

"Scottie," Sophie called out again, "we must've had some kind of earthquake because the frame is on the floor."

"What?" Scottie asked as she walked out of her closet, now clothed in a clean outfit.

Scottie looked at Sophie, who was staring at the table without a frame on it. Sophie then looked at Scottie and said in a hushed voice while pointing at the floor, "Scarlet, look!"

Scottie looked at the picture and both girls watched as the frame began to glow. It was as if a light bulb had turned on within the frame. It turned from deep red to hues of glowing yellow, green, blue, and then orange.

"It reminds me of a flame in a fireplace," Scottie said as she walked toward the frame to pick it up.

"Wait!" Sophie ordered as she caught Scottie's arm to stop her.

Both girls continued to stare at the frame.

"Oh, wow," said Scottie, "I think my eyes are playing tricks on me, but the frame looks bigger."

"It is bigger," Sophie agreed in an excited voice. "This is no ordinary frame. And look, the picture is growing too!"

As the frame grew, it pushed the table back almost against the bedroom door. It continued to glow and change colors as it became larger and larger.

"Oh, my gosh," Sophie shouted, "the frame has grown so much it's touching both walls and is almost touching the ceiling crossbeams."

Just as the plaster on the walls was about to start chipping off, the frame stopped growing. The girls looked at each other, eyes wide open and jaws dropped. They then looked at the frame, which had basically disappeared into the picture.

"This is no ordinary frame," Scottie barely squeaked out, repeating what Sophie had said earlier. "It's, it's . . ."

"Magical," the girls shouted at the same time with shocked voices.

The picture was very clear now. They could see plants with flowers along the road, which almost seemed to run into their bedroom. The hotel across the road had several large archways which made a long porch in front of the building. Under one archway were two heavily carved wooden doors that remained open.

"Listen," Sophie said in a low voice. "You can hear the water splashing in the fountain in front of the hotel!"

"I can hear the birds too," Scottie added. "I can hear something else. Look, it's a horse and rider!"

Both girls gasped as a horse came galloping into the picture on the road, continuing across the picture (almost heading into their bedroom), to the other side of the room, and then out of sight.

"Whew, that was close," Sophie sighed.

"You know what, this is like a drive-in movie, only way more exciting," Scottie exclaimed.

Just as Scottie said that, a colorful parrot with a bright red head and body, brilliant blue tipped wings, and vibrant yellow chest and shoulders flew into the room. Scottie ducked her head as the bird buzzed her hair and landed on the mirror attached to her dresser.

"Don't move," Scottie said with the corner of her mouth to Sophie. "Do you see what I see?"

"Yes!"

Scottie was so close to the parrot that she could almost reach out and touch it. The bird looked right at Scottie, tilted its head in a way that birds do, and then winked. Suddenly, it flew back toward the road, over the fountain, and through the hotel doorway.

"Did you see that?" Scottie asked in an amazed voice. "I could swear that the parrot looked at me and winked before it flew out of here!"

Before Sophie could reply, a beautiful butterfly floated into the room and landed on Sophie's shoulder. She looked at it from the corner of her eye while staying as still as possible and barely breathing. It was black with deep orange round shapes on the larger forewing and yellow round shapes on the lower hindwing sections. It slowly opened and closed its wings while still on Sophie's shoulder. She could see something shimmer or sparkle on the butterfly and realized it was coming from its wings.

Sophie whispered, "Look at the wings."

Scottie nodded her head and said quietly, "I've never seen a butterfly like this before. It's twice the size of the butterflies we see here on the ranch and the wings look like they're covered in glitter."

"I think it's more like crystals or rhinestones," Sophie whispered back.

The butterfly then fluttered off Sophie's shoulder, circled the bedroom, and floated back to the flowers along the road.

The girls looked at each other and Scottie finally said, "I don't know about you, but I want to know what's going on and I think that parrot can lead us to some answers."

"No! No!" Sophie replied in a stern voice. "We can't go out there. It could be dangerous."

"Oh, come on," Scottie complained, "where's your sense of adventure? This must be what Auntie

Jill wants us to do or why would she send us such a magical frame with this picture in it?"

"Well, first let's change into something more appropriate than these shorts," Sophie suggested in a nervous voice. She ran into her closet and then into Scottie's. She had two pairs of cargo capri pants, one in each hand. "Let's wear these pants. You never have enough pockets in a place you know nothing about, and these pants are a little short so we'll stay cool if it's hot."

Both girls leaned into the picture to look up toward the hotel and sky. They could see that it was very sunny with a slight breeze in the air.

"Oh, and we'd better get a light jacket just in case it gets cloudy," Sophie suggested as she pulled Scottie with her so they both would get them out of their closets.

Scottie was the first to walk out of her closet with her capris on too.

"Uh oh, I think we waited too long. LOOK!" Scottie shouted.

Sophie ran out of her closet over to Scottie and looked at the frame. It was already half the size it used to be. Suddenly, the frame began to glow very brightly and in a blink of an eye, it was back to its original size on their bedroom floor in front of the table.

Scottie put her hands on her hips and began to say loudly to Sophie, "Thanks a lot! Because you took so long, the frame couldn't wait anymore!"

"Well," Sophie said with a raised voice and her hands on her hips, "now we know how long we have once the frame grows. Heck, we don't even know what made it grow in the first place. Or maybe it's finished showing us what it can do and won't grow again!"

The girls got really quiet, breathing a little heavily and staring at each other. Then at the same time, they began to laugh.

"This is crazy," Scottie giggled. "Here we are, yelling at each other over a picture frame that glows and grows! Come on, help me move the table back to where it belongs and I'll put the frame back on the table."

After they did this, they continued to put on their socks and shoes to go eat dinner.

"Girls," Ma said as she knocked on their door, "time for dinner. So what did Auntie Jill send you?"

Scottie walked up to Ma and showed her the frame before Sophie could say anything. Amazingly, the frame stayed a silvery color, as if it knew not to change colors or glow when someone other than Scottie or Sophie was in the room.

"Auntie Jill sent us this frame with a pretty picture already in it. Doesn't it look a lot like the ranch?" Sophie commented as she gave Ma the frame.

"It's a pretty frame, but a little boring compared to the other gifts Auntie Jill has given us," Scottie chimed in as Ma held the frame.

"The picture and frame are very nice. You both need to send Auntie Jill a thank you no matter how boring you think it is," Ma said as she put the frame back on the table. "Now then, dinner is ready a little sooner than I thought, so let's eat."

Ma left the room and the girls followed her, being sure to shut their door on the way out.

"Oh, yum, pasta with red sauce!" Scottie exclaimed as she and Sophie sat down next to Pa at the dining table. "Now, hold on," Pa said as he smiled at Ma. "Let's thank the Lord for blessing us with such a wonderful meal."

"And cook!" Sophie blurted out.

After they all ate, the girls helped Ma clear the table. It was all they could do to not run back to their room to see what Auntie Jill's gift was up to.

"What are you girls up to the rest of this fine summer evening?" Pa asked while lighting his pipe.

"Oh, we're going to check on Fuzzy Mama, and since it's so light out, we'll probably brush the horses," Sophie answered while linking arms with Scottie to pull her out of the kitchen.

"All right, girls, have fun but don't get dirty again," Ma said as the girls were already out the kitchen door.

As Sophie and Scottie started walking toward the barn, Scottie suddenly took Sophie's hand and said, "Quick, this way!"

Scottie pulled Sophie so hard that she almost fell to her knees. They walked quickly around the back of the house towards the front door, quietly opened it, and tip-toed down the hallway to their bedroom.

"Gee, Scottie," Sophie said in an irritated voice, "you didn't have to pull me so hard and we should've at least checked on Fuzzy."

"Oh, she's fine," Scottie said in a bossy way.

"Besides, Pa always checks her before the sun goes down. Now open the door. I said, open the door!"

"I'm trying," Sophie answered, "but the door will only open about an inch. I think there's something in the way.

Suddenly, the girls looked at each other and gasped.

"I think I hear a parrot screeching in our room!" Scottie exclaimed in an excited voice.

CHAPTER FOUR

Rancho de Where?

"Quick, Scottie!" Sophie blurted out. "Let's go out the hallway door that leads into the back courtyard. We can then walk over to our back window and crawl through it."

"How do you know it's open?"

"I know because it's summer and Ma always opens our windows in summer to get a cross breeze going in the bedroom to keep it cooler."

"Oh, I don't think I ever noticed," Scottie replied.

They walked quickly through the back courtyard to their bedroom window and started hopping up and down to get a better look inside the room.

Scottie started to laugh, "We must look like two giant Mexican jumping beans that are going crazy!"

Sophie began to laugh, too, and thought the

window was a little high, but they'd have to find a way to crawl into it.

"I know," Scottie began, "why don't you get down on your hands and knees to make a table? Then, I'll stand on your back so I can remove the screen and crawl through the window."

"Wait a minute, why do I have to get all dirty! It's only fair to do 'rock, paper, scissors' to see who has to be the table."

"Okay, okay, but hurry. I can hear that darn bird screeching again!"

The girls began the motions and shouted "rock, paper, scissors!"

Sophie thought for sure Scottie would hold out a rock with her tight fist, so she put her hand out flat in front of her for paper.

"Ha!" Scottie said delightedly. "This time I decided to do scissors," as she made the motion of her fingers cutting Sophie's flat paper hand. "I won, so make a table!"

Sophie rolled her eyes and did as Scottie ordered. "Do you see anything?

"Yes, the picture with the frame is as big as it got before and the parrot is sitting on my headboard preening its feathers! Thank goodness this window is in front of the table in our room."

Scottie jumped up from Sophie's "table." She held onto the frame of the window and pulled herself up to her waist, falling into the room. She then ran over to get a desk chair to stand on and placed it next to the window. She leaned out over the window sill to reach out and pull Sophie up.

"Start jumping and I'll catch your arms to pull you up through the window," Scottie ordered again.

"Ouch, you're squeezing my armpits!" Sophie yelped as Scottie continued to get a tighter grip and pull her through.

Once Sophie landed on the floor and they both got better footing, they were surprised that the parrot wasn't startled. In fact, the bird looked up at them, winked, and continued to clean its wings with its beak.

"Do you think that is the same parrot?" Sophie asked.

"Oh yeah, I'd recognize that wink anywhere!"

"Well, now what?" Sophie wondered out loud.

Scottie looked at Sophie and said in a determined voice, "We walk through the frame, go across the street, pass the fountain, and walk up those stairs that lead to the hotel doors, of course! And we'd better hurry before the frame shrinks back to its normal size again."

Just as she said that, the parrot's bright blue wings began flapping back and forth. Soon it was flying out of the room and, once again, through the hotel doorway.

"All right," Sophie agreed, "but not more than an hour. We won't want to worry Ma and Pa."

Scottie and Sophie linked arms and just as they were stepping off of their hardwood floors and into the picture, Sophie said, "Wait, we'd better get our jackets!"

After she grabbed them, the girls once again linked arms, held their breath, and walked out of their bedroom and onto a dirt trail that led to the road in the

41

picture. After walking about 10 feet, they turned to look back at their bedroom, making sure they could find it. Surprisingly, they could barely see the room because of all the forest plants.

"Let's be sure to find a landmark to remind us of where our room is," Sophie suggested. "There, behind that large fir tree and fern-covered boulder is where our room is, straight out from the hotel fountain and across the street."

It never occurred to them that when they were in their room, they could easily see out into the picture toward the hotel with nothing in the way of their view. So on they walked, crossing the road, passing the fountain, and going up the worn adobe brick stairs to the hotel doorway.

Sophie hesitated a little before walking through the doorway, but once their eyes adjusted from the sunlight to the shadows of the hotel, both girls could see everything in the room. It looked as though they stepped into a large room, probably the hotel lobby where guests could relax out of the hot sun and register for a room. Some guests were sitting at tables, visiting and sipping drinks, while others were standing at a large counter, probably registering for a room Sophie thought. Sophie also noticed a staircase possibly leading to the guest rooms.

"Let's look for the red and blue parrot," Scottie suggested as she linked Sophie's arm and led her toward the guests sitting at the tables.

The girls saw the bird at the same time, sitting on the shoulder of a man at one of the tables studying a large piece of paper. He looked up from the paper and caught Sophie's eye. He immediately began to smile, roll up the paper, and stand up to walk toward them. When he reached the girls, he held out his hand and said with a smile, "Ah, you must be Sophie and you must be Scarlet, I mean, Scottie!" He shook each girl's hand enthusiastically and continued, "We've been expecting you. Welcome to the town of Rancho de La Joya or the Jewell Ranch!"

Both girls were speechless and just looked at him with shocked expressions on their faces.

"Expecting us?" the girls finally questioned at the same time.

"Yes," the man laughed. "I am Dr. Rusty Drake, but you two can call me Uncle Rusty if you like."

"Auntie Jill never told us she'd gotten married. When did this happen?" Sophie asked in a skeptical tone.

"Quite recently," Dr. Drake answered with a smile. "And that is why you are both here. Your Auntie is sorry she couldn't be here to greet you, but she believes that you two can help me."

"Congratulations!" Scottie blurted out as she took his hand and shook it again.

"Yes, congratulations," Sophie said as she offered her hand too. "Now, what kind of help?" Sophie asked hesitantly as she stepped back to observe Dr. Drake.

He was a fairly tall man with a big barrel of a chest and strong-looking arms. He had twinkling blue eyes, a scraggly looking black beard, and a straight pointed nose.

"What I need is help solving a mystery, and I'd like to discuss it more after tea and snacks. So come along and let me show you to your room. I'm sure you girls won't mind sharing." As he started walking toward the stairs, Dr. Drake also said, "Follow me and, oh, be sure to get your packs."

Both girls looked puzzled as they looked around them. Scottie almost jumped as she saw a backpack with her name on it and one with Sophie's name on it set right next to their feet!

"Wow!" Scottie blurted out. "I guess Dr. Drake was expecting us."

The girls quickly picked up their own pack and ran after Dr. Drake, who was already at the top of the stairs and into the hallway. Sophie wasn't quite looking where she was going and when she walked up the stairs, she tripped and bumped into a man who was walking down the stairs. He had long gray hair in a pony tail, a patch over one eye, and wore dark glasses.

"Oh, I'm sorry," Sophie apologized as she was trying to brush off any dirt she possibly got on the man's jacket.

"No harm done, but you might look where you're going in the future," the man said in a gruff voice and then quickly walked out of the hotel.

Dr. Drake stopped at the door with a plaque on it that read Flora Bonita. As he put the key in the lock, the door opened. "That's odd. The maids must have forgotten to lock the door when they finished cleaning the room." He peered into the room and noticed that the room looked clean and safe.

The girls also looked into the room just after Dr. Drake walked in. They saw two beds side by side with bedspreads that had beautiful flowers and butterflies embroidered on them. There was a lamp on the night-stand between the beds. On the other end of the room were a fireplace and a table with two chairs. A door leading to the bathroom was near the table.

"You'll want to use this at night," Dr. Drake said pointing to the fireplace. "It gets awfully chilly when the sun sets around here."

"Oh, wait a minute," Sophie said, getting her courage up. "We can't stay here overnight. In fact, we'd better be going back before Ma and Pa get worried."

"It's all right," Dr. Drake replied as he knelt down before Sophie and Scottie and took their hands. "Time moves at, let's say, a different speed here than on your ranch. And I promise you're safe with me or your Auntie Jill would've never given you the frame." He then stood up and said, "Look through your packs to make sure you two have everything you need. After that, knock on my door, which is right across the hall, and we'll go back down to the hotel's great room for some tea, hot chocolate, and honey cakes. After we've eaten, I'll answer any questions you may have about me, my mystery, and the map."

"What map?" the girls asked at the same time.

"You'll see," Dr. Drake replied as he left their room.

CHAPTER FIVE

Maptrixter

The girls turned to each other after Dr. Drake left the room and shook their heads.

"I can't believe this is happening," Scottie said in a dazed voice. "I guess we should check our packs and then knock on Uncle Rusty's door when we're done."

Each backpack had a couple pairs of socks, undergarments, some shirts, pants, shorts, pajamas, a toothbrush, toothpaste, and a hair brush.

"I guess that's it," Scottie inventoried.

"Wait, I feel a piece of paper in the bottom of my bag," Sophie said as she pulled it out. "It's a note from Auntie Jill."

Dear Girls,

I know that walking through the frame took amazing courage and trust in yourselves and me. I also know that you'll be able to help Dr. Drake, my new husband, in ways that may seem unimaginable to you. Enjoy your adventure.

Love, Auntie Jill

P.S. I'm sure Dr. Drake asked you to call him Uncle Rusty. Call him whatever is most comfortable for you two.

"Gosh, I wonder how she knew we'd come to the hotel?" Scottie asked.

"I don't know, but I'll fold this note back up and put it in my pack."

The girls then left their room to knock on Dr. Drake's door. They could hear the parrot squawk as he walked toward the door to open it. Sure enough, the bird was perched on his shoulder.

"Dr. Drake," Sophie began when the girls stood in front of him, "I hope you don't mind but Scottie and I have decided to call you Dr. Drake until we see Auntie Jill and can congratulate her too on your wedding."

"Why, I don't mind at all," he said with a smile. "If you girls are ready, let's go downstairs and get something to eat."

After they walked into the lobby and past the registration counter, they headed for the great room that had most of the tables. One wall consisted of several giant windows that overlooked the forest and a meadow.

"Where is Rancho de La Joya anyway?" Scottie asked after they sat down and Dr. Drake ordered their drinks and snacks.

"We are in an area of central Mexico that is considered quite sacred," he answered. "Ah, here we are, hot chocolate, tea, and sweet honey cakes. I always say it's hard to talk about anything on an empty stomach!"

As they got their drinks and put what looked like mini cupcakes on their plates, Scottie asked, "What's your parrot's name?"

"Her name is Papaya. I call her that because she'd eat that fruit all day if I let her!"

Both girls giggled.

"Does she go everywhere with you?" Sophie asked.

"Pretty much," he answered. "I found her on one of my travels many years ago. She just showed up on my hotel balcony with papaya in her beak, and we've been together ever since."

"So Papaya adopted you!" Scottie joked and Dr. Drake agreed with a laugh.

As the girls ate their honey cakes, Dr. Drake gave them a jar of honey to add to their cakes to make them even sweeter if they wanted to. Scottie nodded with a smile and took the jar to pour the thick honey on hers. Sophie decided her cake was sweet enough!

"Boy, what would we do without honey bees," he said more to himself than to the girls.

"I love honey!" Scottie said with enthusiasm while pouring more on her cake.

"What are some things that bees do, Scottie?" Dr. Drake asked.

"Well, they make this yummy and sticky honey," she answered with a grin.

"Okay, what else . . . Sophie?"

"They can sting you and it really hurts," she said, rubbing her arm as she remembered the last place she was stung.

"That's true, but they sting only when they are in danger or if their hive is threatened. Another very important thing that bees do is to pollinate plants," Dr. Drake continued. "Are you girls familiar with that term?"

"Oh, sure," Sophie answered, "we've learned about plants and pollination in school. In fact, I know that the pollen is picked up by the bee from the flower's stamen, which looks like thin noodles growing out of the inside of the flower. The pollen then gets carried to the pistil of the same plant or other plants. The stamen noodles surround the pistil, and the pistil holds the cells that the pollen fertilizes. Seeds grow from the fertilized pistil and then new plants grow from the seeds. So I guess without the bees pollinating, most plants would die out," Sophie stated in a matter-of-fact voice.

"Very informative!" Dr. Drake stated in an impressed tone.

"Show off," Scottie said under her breath.

"What did you say?" Dr. Drake asked Scottie.

"Oh, nothing," she replied.

"You know," Dr. Drake began, "bees aren't the only living things that pollinate plants. Birds help to do this, as well as other animals and insects, mostly without them ever knowing what they are doing. In fact, one insect that has made this area of Mexico so special is the butterfly. The butterflies come here to stay for the winter so they can fly all over the world to . . ."

"Pollinate plants also!" Scottie interrupted with authority.

"That is correct, and to find milkweed plants to lay their eggs," Dr. Drake replied with a smile as he looked at Scottie.

"How do you know all of this?" Sophie asked in a curious voice.

"I am, among other things, an entomologist. I study and deal with insects. I've come here because my colleagues and I are concerned about a certain type of butterfly. You see, they seem to be late coming to this area."

"What kind of butterfly?" Sophie asked.

"Speaking of butterflies," Scottie interrupted, "we had a huge one float into our room. It was beautiful and covered with sparkles."

"Crystals," Sophie corrected.

"Are you sure it was a butterfly?" Dr. Drake asked as he leaned forward.

"Oh, yes," Scottie answered. "I was right next to Sophie when it landed on her shoulder."

"Well, I'll be," Dr. Drake said in an amazed voice. "I've heard of the Crystal Creatures but they are considered a legend to the locals. Their stories are passed from generation to generation. The locals here are laughed at when anyone speaks of seeing anything glittering on them. The only creatures this area is known for are the monarch butterflies. And I assure you, they're only covered with pure color and beauty. In fact, millions and millions of them should be here already, but I'm afraid something has happened to them."

"What will happen if they don't show up?" Scottie asked in a concerned voice.

"If they don't migrate to this area, they won't winter here. Then in the month of March, they fly back north to lay their eggs under milkweed plants that eventually become beautiful monarchs. Millions of butterflies and generations of monarchs could be lost. Also, plants will be affected by not getting pollinated, which will also affect animals as well as people over time. I mean the bees can't do it all. Yes, the ecosystem will be in trouble. Therefore, I'm hoping that you girls can help me solve this butterfly mystery."

"A monarch mystery!" the girls cheered at the same time.

"But how can we help?" Sophie asked.

"I'm not sure," Dr. Drake replied, "but I thought we'd start with my map. You see, it just won't cooperate!"

"What do you mean by that?" Sophie asked in a confused tone.

"You see," Dr. Drake began while unrolling the map, "here is the map of this area. You can see the village of Rancho de La Joya and a defined trail to, well, I'm not sure where. It seems that this map leads to nowhere, but it keeps showing up in my duffle bag, my backpack, or my jacket. It wants to be near me but not tell me where to go. I was hoping the map would show me where to find the monarchs if they've fluttered to a new area, but it won't or hasn't yet.

"So you have a map with its own personality," Sophie stated. "That's incredible!"

"Yes, so it seems. I guess as long as it stays with me, I'll have to figure out a way to make it work. Therefore, I've decided that tomorrow after breakfast we'll hike this trail anyway and see what happens." Dr. Drake stated this as if to order the map to shape up.

"That sounds like a great adventure," Scottie agreed as she was finishing her snack.

"Yes, I guess it does too," Sophie also agreed but a little hesitantly.

"Then it's settled. We start early in the morning, so we'd better get to bed," Dr. Drake said as he stood up and rolled up the map.

When they got to their rooms, Dr. Drake told them he'd knock on their door to wake them and that breakfast would follow shortly after that.

"Good night, girls, and remember, I'm right across the hallway if you need me."

Once the girls got ready for bed, they sat next to the fireplace for a while. "Boy," Scottie began, "what a day it's been. I'm really tired now. Let's go to bed so we'll be rested for tomorrow's hike."

Each girl got into her own bed and Scottie turned off the lamp between their beds. All they could see were the embers still glowing in the fireplace. "Wow, it's really dark in this room," Scottie observed while yawning. "Good night, Sis, see you in the morning."

"Good night, Scottie, see you in the morn . . . hey, I thought you turned off the light?"

"I did. It's almost pitch black in here!"

"How can you say that? I can see as if it were as light as day. And look," Sophie continued as she got out of bed, "there's something on the table. Oh, my gosh!"

"What is it?" Scottie asked as she reached to turn on the lamp.

"It's the map!" Sophie almost shouted.

Scottie ran over to the table and then looked at Sophie and gasped.

"What's wrong?" Sophie asked in a concerned voice.

"It's, it's your eyes. They look like a cat's eyeballs with narrow slits."

"Quick, hand me a mirror," Sophie demanded.

Scottie found one in her backpack and handed it to Sophie. Sure enough, she could see that her eyes had narrow slits in them, just like a cat's. But, as the light stayed on, they went back to normal.

"This is creepy," Scottie said. "First, we find the map unrolled on our table and then we find out you can see in complete darkness."

"Turn off the lamp again to see if I can see in the dark."

After her eyes adjusted, Sophie could see everything as if the lamp was still on. Her eyes didn't feel any different, so she walked over to the map. As she sat down next to it, the map slid over next to her, which made her jump out of the chair.

"What is it?" Scottie asked as she quickly turned on the lamp. She walked toward Sophie, who was pointing at the map.

"I think the map likes me. It moved toward me, and look, the trail to nowhere is glowing!"

"Let me see. Oh, wow, we'd better take Maptrixter

over to Dr. Drake to show him that we have it, and to tell him our, uh, discovery about you."

"Maptrixter?" Sophie asked.

"Well, I figured if the map is going to be with us now, we might as well name it."

"Makes sense to me," Sophie replied.

Sophie then carefully rolled up the map and both girls quietly peered out their door to make sure no one was in the hallway. They then quickly tip-toed across the hallway and knocked on Dr. Drake's door.

CHAPTER SIX

The Hike

"Who's pounding on my door?" The girls could hear Dr. Drake as he unlocked and opened it.

"Dr. Drake! Dr. Drake!" Both girls were chanting in a loud whisper as his hotel room door opened. Dr. Drake could tell that something wasn't right. Sophie and Scottie looked excited and scared at the same time.

"We have something that is yours," Sophie announced as she handed the rolled-up map to him.

"Well, well. So the map followed you this time. It looks like this map is now yours," he said in a rather amused tone.

"We've named it Maptrixter and there's something else," Scottie added as Dr. Drake shuttled them into his room and closed the door. "We've also learned something about Sophie. It got really dark after I turned off the lamp next to our beds and about one minute later Sophie asked me to turn off the lamp again. That's when we discovered that . . ."

"We discovered that I can see perfectly in the dark, like a cat!" Sophie blurted out before Scottie could finish her story.

"Your Auntie Jill told me you both were special, but I didn't realize she meant this type of special, as in special powers or talents. Sophie, let me see your eyes."

Dr. Drake took out a pen, or at least it looked like one, from his backpack. He pressed the end of it and a mini light turned on at the opposite end of the pen. He aimed the light into each of Sophie's eyes.

"Does this hurt your eyes or give you a sudden headache?"

"No," she answered.

"Well, then, I believe it was meant to be. Your new, uh, night vision may come in handy, so if you're not bothered by this, I'm sure you'll be fine. But let's keep this new found ability between us, okay?"

"Sounds good to me," Scottie agreed with a yawn. "I think we'd better get some sleep now. I have a feeling that tomorrow is going to be very eventful."

"Good idea," Dr. Drake said. "Now, Sophie, try not to worry about your new talent and focus on getting a good night's sleep." He turned each girl toward the door and as they stepped into the hallway, he handed back the map to Sophie. "I'm sure you'll have a lot more success with this than I did! Good night, girls, and I'll see you bright and early in the morning."

The girls had kept their door slightly opened when they knocked on Dr. Drake's door. This allowed them to get back into their room easily.

"Dr. Drake seemed okay about your eyes and about Maptrixter choosing you," Scottie observed as she got into bed.

"Yeah, maybe Maptrixter will help us on our hike tomorrow. Good night, Scottie. Be sure to say a prayer for Ma and Pa before you go to sleep. Heck, say one for us too!"

In the morning, just as the sun was rising, Dr. Drake knocked on their door with Papaya on his shoulder, and they all went down to the great room for breakfast. Once they ordered their food, a young man from the village walked up to their table.

"Ah, Senior Vargas," Dr. Drake said as he stood up and shook his hand. "Sophie, Scottie, this is Diego Vargas and he will be helping us with our packs and food on our journey."

"Por favor," Senior Vargas said as he shook each girl's hand, "call me Diego." He spoke English with a thick accent that the girls understood just fine. "After all of you finish eating, meet me out by the fountain. I have all of your backpacks ready to go."

"Very good, Diego, gracias," Dr. Drake replied as Diego walked out of the great room and toward the fountain and supplies.

"We need someone to help us carry our stuff," Scottie said in an excited voice. "I can't wait to get going!"

"Is Diego from around here?" Sophie asked Dr. Drake.

"Yes, he grew up in this valley and is very excited

about what our hike may bring. You see, your story of the crystal butterfly got around the village rather quickly last night. Diego would also like to find the lost monarchs. Diego is sure they're here somewhere and wants to find out, like me, what has happened to them."

After they ate their eggs, tortillas, and sweet mango, they left the hotel to meet Diego at the fountain. Each of the hikers had a backpack of clothes, a bed roll, and a water canteen. Dr. Drake and Diego also carried the food and tents.

"You've got the map, Sophie?" Dr. Drake asked.

"I've got it right in my pack," she answered.

"Good, then let's get to the trail. No need to look at the map for now. I know the 'trail to nowhere' by memory," Dr. Drake said with a sigh.

As the group hiked on the trail, they saw huge pine trees, ferns, a few wild flowers, squirrels, and some deer. The dogwood trees were changing colors and birds were flying and chirping everywhere. Some had red chests, and others had blue wings with yellow heads.

"Is it autumn here?" Sophie asked.

"Yes, but winter is almost here," Dr. Drake replied.

"Wow, it never occurred to me that we'd be in another season than the one at home," Sophie commented as they continued to hike.

Diego had gone up ahead and came back to let them know he found a clearing along the trail, which was also next to a bubbling creek.

"What a great location for lunch. Well done, Diego," Dr. Drake stated as he helped the girls walk over some boulders to get to the clearing. "Now, how are you girls doing?" He asked as he took off his backpack and began feeding Papaya some dried fruit and crackers.

"I'm fine," Scottie answered. "How about you, Sis?"

"I'm okay. Just a little tired I guess. What's for lunch?"

Diego spread out a multicolored striped blanket and set out cheeses, dried meats, tortillas, grapes, and what looked like sugar cookies. "It's simple," Diego described, "but the food travels well and tastes good too."

"It looks great," both girls announced as they began to reach for their lunch.

While they all ate, Scottie noticed something floating along the edge of the creek. She walked down the sandy slope to pick it up with her hand and brought it over to Dr. Drake.

"Is this a monarch butterfly?" Scottie asked.

"Yes, it is. Where did you find it?"

"Floating in the creek."

"Well, it seems this one didn't have much of a chance. But since it was floating downstream, we're on the right track to continue on this trail walking north. If everyone is finished eating lunch," Dr. Drake continued, "we should pack up. I want to reach the end of the trail that's shown on the map by sundown. There's supposed to be a full moon tonight, which will make setting up camp a lot easier."

Sophie looked at Maptrixter just before they started heading north on the trail again. She wanted to make sure they were headed on the right trail as Dr. Drake described, and sure enough, the map showed the trail next to the creek.

She rolled "the Trixter," as she nicknamed the map, back up and put it carefully in her backpack. As they continued to hike, the creek seemed to get further and further away from the trail. Soon all anyone could see was forest again. The trail seemed suddenly to turn sharply to the left, and they found themselves walking along a rather wide and slow-flowing river. Diego noticed Scottie looking at the water.

"We call this the Lazy River. We were walking along one of its creeks back there on the trail," Diego informed her.

"Oh," Scottie replied, "it looks refreshing."

"Yes, it does, but the water is very cold right now, about 55 degrees. The river is too cold for swimming, but great for fishing. That is how we will eat dinner tonight," Diego said with a smile.

"You mean we have to fish?" Sophie asked.

"Why sure, haven't you ever fished before?" Diego said to both girls with a surprised look.

"Not really. We don't have a lot of rivers where our ranch is," Scottie replied.

"Then it's settled. You and Sophie will help me catch dinner!"

Time passed and Dr. Drake finally stopped the group. "We'll set up camp here. As you can see, the trail forks here, with both trails looking rather overgrown. We'll have to choose which one to take tomorrow. The map seems to stop right here."

As Dr Drake said that, Sophie reached in to get the Trixter and unrolled it. Dr. Drake was right; the trail just ended where they were standing.

"Good," Diego stated. "I'll set up the fishing poles and the girls can help me fish."

"Oh, great," Sophie replied in a sarcastic tone, "this should be really interesting."

There was plenty of sunlight, so Diego decided he would set out the tent supplies after they caught their dinner. He showed the girls how to bait their hooks and cast the fishing lines using their poles.

Scottie wasn't paying much attention when her pole almost jumped out of her hands. "Oh! Oh! I think I've caught something. What do I do?"

Diego quickly ran over and showed her how to slowly tip up the pole while holding onto the reel. He then helped her to turn the reel very slowly, which brought the fishing line toward them, bringing the fish closer too.

"Muy bueno!" Diego shouted. "This fish is almost 2 feet long!" He took the fish off the hook and put it into a mini pond of water that he'd made so the fish couldn't swim away. "A few more of these and we'll be eating dinner in no time at all."

Diego caught three more fish. Sophie caught one, but they decided it was too small and carefully took it off the hook and threw it back into the river. Sophie was relieved; she didn't think she could eat anything that she'd caught anyway.

As they fished, Dr. Drake put out the tents so Diego could easily set them up, and then pulled out a pad of paper to write down some notes. He walked about 20 yards down one of the weedy trails to see if he could find any clues to where the monarchs might be. After fishing, the girls set up their tent with some help from Diego. They then rolled out their bedding and brought in their packs as well.

Sophie noticed that Dr. Drake favored one trail over the other and decided she would check it out later. She also noticed that the fish smelled really yummy as Diego cooked it!

"Diego, you've out done yourself again!" Dr. Drake announced. "This fish tastes excellent and the mango salsa tastes perfect on it too."

The girls agreed. They'd never eaten fish with salsa and it was good. Diego also gave the girls ice-cold water from the river to drink, which completely quenched their thirst. For dessert, they had thick chocolate cake that resembled brownies from home, and they all sat around the camp fire as the night fell upon them.

Dr. Drake gave each girl a flashlight so they could easily see in the dark. This light also kept Sophie's eyes from changing, which was a good thing since Diego didn't know about her special night vision yet.

"I think we're going to go to bed now," Sophie called out to Dr. Drake and Diego from their tent.

"Good night, girls," both men replied.

"The birds will wake you two bright and early, so it's a good idea to get some sleep," Diego called out to them.

"I think I'll get some sleep too," Dr. Drake said to Diego as he patted him on the shoulder.

"Good night, doc. See you in the morning," Diego replied with a yawn.

Neither of them noticed Sophie's head sticking out from her tent and looking toward the moonlit sky.

CHAPTER SEVEN

Glitter

The moon hadn't quite risen yet, but that didn't bother Sophie as she looked up at the sky. She turned to look at Scottie, who was fast asleep. She decided to lie back down on her sleeping bag too, but she just stared up at the tent, eyes wide open. Sophie kept thinking about the trail that Dr. Drake walked on while Diego, Scottie, and she were fishing for dinner. I've got to check that trail out, she thought to herself.

"Maptrixter," she said under her breath, "we're going for a walk."

Sophie quietly put on her hiking boots, grabbed a sweatshirt and the map from her pack, and crawled out of her tent. Everyone was asleep. She noticed that Diego was sleeping close to the dimming flames of the camp fire, not in a tent like the rest of them. She carefully walked past him, making sure not to make a sound. As Sophie began to walk on the weedy trail, she felt as if this wasn't the right way, but decided to give it a try. Heck, Sophie wasn't even sure what to look for on the trail anyway. She stopped and unrolled Maptrixter to study it. She could see the trail that she was walking on, but nothing else was showing up on the map. After walking a few more yards, Sophie decided to turn around and head back to camp. I can't believe I'm doing this, she thought. I'm usually the one to stay back and watch everyone else explore or try new things first. As she turned around, Sophie heard a swooping noise and started to duck out of the way when, all of a sudden, she felt something on her shoulder. It was Papaya!

"Oh, my gosh, Papaya," she whispered almost out of breath, "you nearly scared me half to death! I guess we'll turn back to camp. It looks like Trixter doesn't want to cooperate with me either."

Sophie kept Maptrixter open as she walked on the trail back to camp with Papaya still on her shoulder. She was hoping that the map would show her something, but nothing seemed to change. As she neared her tent, Sophie let out a big sigh and started to roll Maptrixter up and shoo Papaya back to Dr. Drake's tent.

Suddenly, something started to happen to the map. It began to get thicker and very stiff, like a square piece of wood!

"I, I guess we're not done exploring the trails after all," Sophie said to Papaya in a slightly shaky voice.

"But which way do I go?" she whispered to herself and to the parrot. "I know, I'll go on this other trail that is barely visible and see if Trixter shows any changes."

As Sophie began to walk, the map began to become like paper again, no, more like cloth or burlap. So she decided to hike further on the trail.

"I'm glad you're here with me, Papaya. It makes me feel not so alone." As she said this, she could have sworn that Papaya winked at her.

Sophie stopped to look at Maptrixter again and gasped! Each step she took was now showing up on the map. It looked like a mini shoe print that glowed. Now we're getting somewhere, Sophie thought with a smile. After walking about 50 yards, she came upon a very steep cliff wall with giant boulders. She estimated that this rock wall must be 300 feet tall. Bushes and trees were growing out through the cracks in the wall. Sophie looked at the map and the footsteps were still showing up!

"Now, Trixter, Papaya and I can't very well climb this wall of rocks or walk through it," Sophie said while looking at the boulders. So she began to walk left, but the footsteps disappeared. She then started to the right, and still no footsteps. Sophie put her hands in the air out of frustration while holding the map and decided to turn around and go back to camp. She then noticed something on Maptrixter. She blinked several times, thinking that her night vision was playing tricks on her. She noticed that the rock wall was glowing. After looking at Papaya, she also noticed something on its beak.

"Why, Papaya, you have something shiny on your beak. Here, let me rub it off." Sophie gently tried to wipe it from the parrot's beak, but it was still there.

"Well, I'll be, this shiny thing is like a tiny piece of crystal." It then occurred to Sophie that the shimmer from the crystal was like that of the giant butterfly that floated into her room.

"Oh, wow, Papaya! Could we be near where the crystal creatures live that Diego talked about? If we are, I think it's starting to affect your beak."

Just as she said that, Papaya began to flap her wings and fly, at first toward their camp. The parrot then turned around and headed straight for the rock wall!

"Stop, Papaya, stop!" Sophie shouted. But it kept flying toward the boulders. Sophie dropped Maptrixter and covered her eyes with her hands, waiting for a loud thump, but the sound never came. With her night vision, Sophie looked all over the boulder wall for Papaya, but the parrot couldn't be found. She picked up Maptrixter and looked for any new directions. Her footprints were still showing, and to her surprise, Papaya's wing span now appeared on the map, right next to the wall!

This is crazy, Sophie thought. So she rolled Maptrixter up and pointed it toward the wall, like it was a sword. As she did this, the sword became stiff as well. She then began to walk, no shuffle her feet, carefully toward the boulders. She held her breath as she got closer, waiting for impact. To her amazement, she and the map were able to walk right through the wall. It was as if the giant boulders weren't even there! Sophie immediately turned around and could see the weedy trail that she was on. The moon was now higher in the night sky, which allowed Sophie to see even better. The trail now led to what looked like a hedge of thorns about 10 feet tall.

"Papaya? Papaya? Where are you?"

Sophie heard a squawk on the other side of the hedge. She looked on Maptrixter and sure enough, the hedge was now on the map, and showing up also on the map was Papaya just on the other side of the hedge!

"Oh, great," Sophie exclaimed to Maptrixter, "I can't fly over all of these thorns like Papaya did. So now what?"

A glowing dot began to get very bright on the map that coincided with where Sophie was standing. So she began to look around and noticed a small opening on the bottom of the hedge. She squatted down and began to crawl on her hands and knees under the thorns, being very careful not to get snagged by the sharp edges. She crawled through the opening and found herself in some kind of room. As her eyes adjusted, she realized that she was in a large tunnel. It seemed to be about 10 feet wide with a ceiling that was about 10 feet high. As she looked around, she noticed that light was shimmering on the walls all around her. She wasn't sure what the walls were covered with, but she did know that it was beautiful.

Sophie kept walking for a while and said to Maptrixter in a low voice, "This is nothing like the ranch. Heck, I don't think I'm even in the frame or Mexico anymore."

"Oh, don't be silly," said a voice ahead of her. "Of course, you're still in Mexico."

"Papaya, was that you?" Sophie asked in a startled voice, her eyes opened wide. She continued to walk toward the voice and found herself out of the tunnel and into a clearing, like a meadow, which was next to a body of water shimmering from the moonlight.

"Oh, no, she's not talking. I am."

Just then Sophie jumped back and a saw a beautiful multicolored bird, a toucan she thought. It was perched high on a branch of an enormous banyan tree. It sat there, lifting an ebony wing and preening itself with a large lime green beak with an orange stripe on it and a bright red tip at the end. Its eyes were black with aqua blue circling each eye, and then bright yellow circling the blue, and then orange circling around the yellow. The toucan's body was black with tail feathers that looked like they were dipped in white paint. Sophie gasped when the bird put its wing down and looked at her. The moonlight danced off of every feather, making the toucan look as if it were covered in glitter from tail feather to beak!

"Come closer, my dear. Have you never seen a toucan before?" He kept talking, not really waiting for Sophie to answer. "My name is Tomas and I am the observer and communicator of this land. Welcome to the Crystal Canyon!"

Sophie slowly walked closer to the tree and to Tomas.

"We thought you'd never find the tunnel, but Maptrixter, as you call it, came through for us. Gracias, Maptrixter, for your help!"

Maptrixter twirled in Sophie's hand several times as if to say you're welcome!

"Maptrixter wanted me to find the Crystal Canyon?" Sophie asked Tomas, almost forgetting that she was talking to a toucan.

"Yes, you see, we need help from you and your friends. We've been hoping to find the right person to enter our canyon first. After our scout landed on your shoulder, we knew that you and your sister would be the perfect choice."

"You mean the giant butterfly that floated into my bedroom was all part of a plan?"

"It took me a little while to convince Tomas, but we knew that Bella is never wrong when she lands on something or someone."

"Who said that?" Sophie blurted out as she quickly turned to her right to look along the shoreline of the sparking lake. Just then, a very large creature walked out from under the bushes and stopped to take a drink. From what Sophie could see, it looked like a large cat with the face and shoulders of a cheetah, but the rest of its body similar to a tiger.

"This is Jinx," Tomas said. "He is our, uh, our security guard and knows every inch of this canyon and the land around it. No doubt your guide, Diego, has seen him every now and then, thinking his eyes were playing tricks on him. Jinx likes to tease humans when he's bored. First they will see him, and then Jinx will disappear into the canyon, leaving them staring at nothing while scratching their heads. We call him Jinx because it seems to suit him quite well."

Sophie just stared at Jinx. He was as big as a Great Dane dog and his fur shimmered in the moonlight.

"Why, thank you, Tomas, for such a kind introduction," Jinx commented. "We decided to let you come first from your group, Sophie, because of your night vision abilities and your calm nature. I'm sure, as is To-mas, that you're a little stunned right now. But, please, look around and see how special this land is. We are concerned, as is Dr. Drake, where the butterflies are. When the monarchs and other butterflies and insects come here, they pollinate the entire canyon, as well as lay their eggs here and beyond our borders all over the world. We're hoping that with your help we'll be able to find the missing monarchs."

"Yes," Tomas began to say, "Jinx and the humming-birds have noticed some human activity on the remote outer trails around the canyon, and we think those people could have something to do with the mon-archs' disappearance."

As Jinx and Tomas were talking, Sophie did what Jinx suggested and looked around. She could see a huge lake in the middle of the Crystal Canyon. There was a beautiful waterfall cascading down into the lake from the canyon walls that must have been 200 feet high. The tunnel must've taken me to the canyon floor, Sophie thought. She noticed that the flowers and trees were twice the size of any she'd seen at the ranch or on the trails they'd been hiking on during the day. The colors were brilliant green, yellow, red, orange, and more. I can't wait to see the canyon in daylight, she thought.

"Oh, my," Sophie blurted out, "I've got to get back to camp before the sun rises! If Scottie wakes up and notices I'm gone, she'll wake Dr. Drake and Diego, and then they'll all be searching for me."

"You're right, Sophie," Tomas agreed. "Will you help us and bring the rest of your group to this canyon?"

"I'm still in a little shock about this place, but yes, I'll do whatever I can to help."

"Good, then let's get you back to camp." Tomas clapped his wings and two hummingbirds flew over her head faster than she'd ever seen. Tomas said to them, "Escort Sophie back to the trail." He then turned to Sophie. "The hummers will wait for you at the front of the boulders tomorrow morning. Please don't say anything to the others about us and describe few details about the canyon. Just show Maptrixter to Dr. Drake. He'll see your footsteps appear on the map and will follow you without too much hesitation, but with lots of questions, I'm sure."

"Why wouldn't Maptrixter cooperate with Dr. Drake?" Sophie asked.

"Because, my dear, Maptrixter and I were waiting for you!" Tomas answered with a twinkle in his eye.

Sophie smiled and then noticed one of the hummingbirds flying just in front of her. The other one flew in so fast that it accidentally bumped into the other one, which was then bounced into the tree branches. Sophie couldn't help but giggle.

"You'll have to excuse Paco. He's so fast that sometimes he can't control himself," Tomas said in a sarcastic tone.

"I see," Sophie commented with a smile, "and where's . . ."

"Poncho is the other one," Tomas continued. "You can tell them apart because Poncho has a bright blue feathered neck and Paco's is bright green."

"They're kind of shifty if you ask me," Jinx said.

73

"But they can fly ahead and let me know what's over the ridge or around the next turn in a road or trail."

Once Poncho flew back from being bounced into the trees, the hummers buzzed Sophie's head to let her know it was time to go. They all headed for the tunnel, which would lead back to the outer trail.

"Now, remember, Sophie," Tomas shouted as she was entering the tunnel, "just use Maptrixter and Dr. Drake, Diego, and Scottie will follow you. Tell them as little as possible until you get to the tunnel. Then, for starters, you can tell them about me!"

"Okay, Tomas, I'll see you in the morning," Sophie replied. "Papaya, Papaya, we've got to go," she yelled while cupping her hand next to her mouth to make her voice louder. Just then, the parrot swooped down from a nearby tree and landed on her shoulder. Sophie noticed her beak had another crystal on it. This canyon sure does affect the animals, she thought while walking.

"I hope Dr. Drake won't notice your beak until I have a chance to explain the crystal when we reach the tunnel opening," Sophie said to Papaya, half expecting the parrot to reply to her as she looked around for Paco and Poncho.

CHAPTER EIGHT

Back Track

Paco and Poncho tried their best to fly slowly so Sophie could keep up as she walked back to the tunnel entrance.

"This is so strange," Sophie said to Papaya. "I know we're walking up hill in this tunnel, but I'm not even breathing hard or getting tired. I think this place is magical."

The tunnel seemed to sparkle as she walked to the entrance. When she walked out, she noticed that the hummers had shown her a different way out, about 30 feet from where she had entered when holding Maptrixter out in front of her. I guess this keeps others from seeing you leave through the boulders, Sophie thought to herself. Poncho and Paco showed Sophie how to get to the weedy trail, just around a large bush. She had to look down on the trail to keep from tripping or sliding on the pebbles laced among the weeds of the trail. Suddenly, Sophie looked up and stopped just before she ran into something.

"Sophie, where have you been? It's past midnight!" Dr. Drake asked in a loud and concerned voice.

"Oh, you scared me!" Sophie replied. "I, I decided to take a walk since I have this great new vision. I also thought that maybe the Trixter would cooperate with me if I was alone."

"Well, obviously Maptrixter decided not to," Dr. Drake said with a sarcastic tone. "You could've gotten lost, Sophie. This was very dangerous of you to leave the camp by yourself."

"I know it was, but Papaya was with me so I thought if I was in danger, she could fly to the camp to get you."

"Hmm, that sounds logical in a strange sort of way, but don't do it again, okay?"

Just then, Poncho and Paco flew down and buzzed around Dr. Drake's head and then disappeared as fast as they had appeared.

"What was that?" Dr. Drake yelled as he instinctively ducked out of the way.

"I think they were hummingbirds," Sophie knowingly answered.

"Now, that's odd," Dr. Drake commented. "I guess with the full moon, animals have a tendency to do strange things and not act normally."

"I think you're right, Dr. Drake. I don't think there's anything normal about this place!"

"Let's get going back to camp," Dr. Drake ordered, with Papaya now on his shoulder. He kept Sophie just a little ahead of him to keep an eye on her until they got back.

Sophie said good night to him as she quietly slipped into her tent and sleeping bag. Sophie could barely believe what she had just seen and experienced in the Crystal Canyon. Sophie looked at Scottie, who was sound asleep. I'm not sure how I'm supposed to get Dr. Drake and the others to follow me back. I guess I'll figure it out in the morning, she thought. Sophie yawned, settled into her sleeping bag, and fell fast asleep.

CHAPTER NINE

Trails and Tunnels

S cottie could hear all sorts of noises coming from outside the tent, so she decided to get dressed and see what all the commotion was about. As Scottie stepped out of the tent, she looked up to see Diego chasing a deer away from the camp, his arms flapping like a bird trying to take flight!

"Get away from my granola!" Diego shouted as he ran toward the bags of food and the deer.

Scottie giggled to herself and ran over to help him. They both continued to flap their arms and chase not one but three deer away from the food bags.

"It looks like all of the food is still here," Diego said as he inspected the bags. "Gracias, Scottie, for helping me to scare those deer away. You never know what we'll run into in this wilderness."

"I was happy to help, Diego. I'll go wake up Sophie so we can help you with breakfast." Just as Scottie was walking toward her tent, Sophie poked her head out of the opening. She yawned and rubbed her eyes as she waved to Scottie. Scottie motioned her to come out of the tent. Sophie got dressed, put on her hiking boots, and joined Scottie around the low flames of the camp fire.

"Boy, did I sleep well," Scottie announced to Sophie. "How about you?"

"Oh, I slept okay, but I had some really weird dreams," Sophie answered as she gazed at the flames. When she looked up, Sophie saw Dr. Drake and Papaya coming out of his tent. She instantly remembered that her night hike wasn't a dream and that she knew she had some explaining to do to Dr. Drake.

"Good morning, girls," Dr. Drake greeted as he looked at Sophie. "We'd better get some breakfast before we decide which way to go on the trail from here. Do you still have the map, Sophie?"

"Oh, yes, it's in the tent."

"Good, we'll need it for a reference and maybe even some guidance today," Dr. Drake said in a stern voice.

"Oh, I told Diego that we'd help him set up breakfast. Come on, Sophie, let's go," Scottie suggested as she pulled Sophie toward where Diego was setting up the food.

"Boy," Scottie whispered as they walked toward Diego, "Dr. Drake sure is in a grumpy mood this morning. Here, Diego, let us help you," Scottie said as they both started to pass around the granola, dried fruit, and tortillas.

They all took their food and sat on some rocks near the camp fire. "Diego, that was great!" Dr. Drake commented about the food. "In fact, I think I'll get more granola for the hike ahead. Sophie, why don't you get some for Scottie and you to share?"

"Good idea," Sophie agreed and stood up to follow Dr. Drake.

"Now, Sophie, we need to talk about last night," Dr. Drake said to her as they both reached for the granola to put into small brown paper bags.

"I know, Dr. Drake, I promise to tell you everything when we're on our way. The overgrown trail that you found me on last night is the way we should hike. Maptrixter and I will prove it to you if you'll give us a chance."

"Well, I guess it can't hurt to hike that way for a little while. But if we wind up going nowhere because the trail is too difficult, you have to promise me we'll turn around without any complaints."

"I promise!" Sophie said with a big grin. Just then, something flew by her head so fast that she could barely tell what it was.

"It's those darn hummingbirds from last night!" Dr. Drake exclaimed. "Why on earth would they come so close to you?" Dr. Drake's eyes narrowed as if he just figured something out. "I think we should pack up and get going, don't you Sophie?"

"Yes, Dr. Drake, that's a very good idea," Sophie replied as she stepped back and ran to get Scottie to pack up their belongings and take down their tent.

"Hey, Sophie," Scottie said in a confused tone of voice while she was re-packing her things. "Look what I found." She took her hand out from the bottom of her pack, holding a small box.

"How weird!" Sophie exclaimed. "I wonder how your rain box got in your backpack. It looks smaller than I remember."

"Check your pack to see if you have yours," Scottie suggested.

Sophie reached into her pack and felt a box on the bottom of it. She pulled it out, and sure enough, it was her box, and smaller too.

"I wonder if they got smaller coming through the frame," Sophie commented.

"This is strange."

"What's strange?" Sophie asked.

"I have a shiny new quarter in mine, and it just fits into the box," Scottie answered. "I think I'll put it into one of the pockets of my cargo pants for safe keeping. Look to see if you have anything in your box, Sophie."

"Nope, mine's empty."

"I'm not sure why we have these rain boxes in our packs," Sophie observed, "but we'd better put them back and keep packing."

"I don't know why either, Sis, but at least they're small because my pack can't fit another thing in it." Scottie grunted as she lifted her pack and put it on a rock so they could take down their tent.

With their backpacks ready to go, Sophie made sure Maptrixter was easily accessible in hers. Diego was still packing a few things, so the girls started to walk over to help him.

"Oh, my gosh," Scottie blurted out, "I think I see a striped snake behind that pine tree! Let's go check it out."

Just as Scottie started to walk toward the tree,

Sophie noticed Poncho and Paco flying very close to the tree. She then gasped. That's no snake, she thought. That's Jinx's tail!

"Wait, Scottie!" Sophie shouted. "It could be dangerous. Go get Diego first."

As Scottie turned to get Diego, the tail disappeared in the blink of an eye.

"Whew," Sophie said with a sigh, "I think it's gone now. Let's not bother Diego and get our backpacks."

Dr. Drake and Diego were ready to get started. With Maptrixter securely in Sophie's pack, the group started their hike on the weedy trail, which was very uneven and full of loose pebbles. After hiking for a while, Sophie decided that she should check Maptrixter.

"I think we should stop here so I can look on Trixter," Sophie told the others as she took her backpack off and pulled it out. Sophie didn't realize it, but she was barely breathing as she unrolled the map, uncertain what she was about to see.

"Look everyone, our footsteps are showing up on the map! This is definitely the way to go," Sophie said with a smile.

Dr. Drake looked over Sophie's shoulder to see for himself.

"Well, I'll be," Dr. Drake commented while tipping his hat back to scratch his forehead. "I guess this darn map did cooperate after all."

"Wait, let me see!" Scottie blurted out. She almost knocked Sophie over as she peered over the map. "Is this some kind of trick?"

"No, Scottie, this is real and I can't explain it either," Dr. Drake replied.

Sophie smiled. "Shall we continue to hike on this trail?"

All of them nodded yes while they got a drink from their canteens.

As the group hiked closer to the giant boulder wall, Sophie knew she'd have to be on the lookout for Poncho and Paco. At about 50 yards from the rock wall, the hummingbirds buzzed their heads. All of them instinctively ducked, as if to avoid hitting a low-growing branch from the surrounding trees. Suddenly, both birds stopped and hovered like helicopters right in front of Sophie's face, and then slowly began to rise.

"What are those hummingbirds doing?" Scottie asked in a low voice while looking at the birds and then at Sophie. Scottie then began to reach for Paco, but Sophie quickly grabbed her hand.

"These birds are here to guide us further on the trail," Sophie explained, looking at Scottie and then the others. "I, um, met them last night. What they want us to do is look around to be sure that no one else sees us as we continue on this trail."

"Their colors are so bright. Es muy bonita!" Diego observed.

"The one with the shimmering blue neck is Poncho, and Paco has the neon green neck."

"That's crazy, loco!" Diego blurted out. "How could you possibly know their names?"

Just as Diego asked that, Poncho and Paco darted past him and out of sight.

"Because," Sophie began to explain, "Tomas told me."

"Who's Tomas?" Dr. Drake asked in a concerned voice. "It sounds like you had quite an adventure last night," he stated before Sophie could answer.

"Adventure?" Scottie almost shouted. "You mean I slept through all of this?"

"I promise I'll answer all of your questions, but we really need to keep going before somebody sees us," Sophie said as she began to walk again.

"Now, Scottie," Sophie said in a low voice as they continued to hike, "I'm going to need you to do as I say and follow my directions. This way, Dr. Drake and Diego will follow too."

Scottie nodded. As they got closer to the boulders, Sophie held out the rolled up Maptrixter. It began to transform into what seemed like a long wooden stick or sword as it had the night before.

"Scottie," Sophie almost shouted, "I need you to put your hand on my shoulder and continue walking just behind me. Diego, you need to put your hand on Scottie's shoulder, and Dr. Drake, put your hand on Diego's shoulder." Sophie turned to look from one to the other, who were now in a line behind her. "Our footsteps are on Maptrixter, so please trust and follow me and we'll be fine."

They all nodded and agreed to follow Sophie, walking straight for the giant boulder wall!

"Now everyone, keep your eyes forward and keep walking," Sophie instructed. As they did this, they could feel the trail under their feet change to a smooth surface. They were now within the boulder walls.

"Okay, now you can look around," Sophie said excitedly.

Dr. Drake and the others looked around and could see they were now on the other side of the wall, with the weedy trail behind them lit up by the morning sun. Looking in amazement at one another, they also noticed the smooth trail at their feet. It was shaded where they stood, but not too dark to see.

"We now need to walk toward a large hedge with giant thorns on it," Sophie directed. "Wait, let me get my bearings," Sophie said as she rolled out the now soft Maptrixter. "Yes, here we are, and this is the opening," she excitedly announced. "We need to crouch down and crawl through this space. It seems small, but we all can fit. Just crawl through slowly to avoid getting snagged by the thorns."

"Wow, Sis, how could you find this?" Scottie asked in amazement.

"I couldn't have found any of this without the Trixter's help."

Just as Sophie said this, Papaya began to flap her wings and fly from Dr. Drake's shoulder over the 10-foot hedge and out of sight.

"Papaya!" Dr. Drake shouted.

"It's all right, Dr. Drake. Papaya knows where she is going," Sophie said as she began to crawl through the opening.

When everyone in the group had crawled through to the other side of the hedge, only Sophie's eyes could adjust to the darkness. She spotted two thick branches about 3 feet long with twine wrapped around the tops of them. They were set in the cracks of the walls in the tunnel. Dr. Drake pulled out his flashlight to see where they were.

"If you have some matches, Dr. Drake, we can light the torches that have been placed on either side of the tunnel," Sophie suggested as she directed his flashlight beam to where the torches were.

"Here, I've got the matches," Diego offered as he reached into his outer pack pocket to hand them to Dr. Drake.

Diego pulled the torches from their crevice and Dr. Drake lit them. It didn't take long for them to burn brighter and brighter as the minutes went by. The light was much brighter than the flashlight's beam.

"I guess I won't need this anymore," Dr. Drake stated as he put his flashlight back into his pack.

"According to Maptrixter, we need to walk through this tunnel to the other end," Sophie said after looking at the map and rolling it up again.

As they all walked through the tunnel, they began to notice that the flames made the walls sparkle in brilliant colors.

"Wow!" Scottie exclaimed. "This reminds me of the glitter we used in school art projects, but way prettier."

"Yeah, me too," Sophie agreed. "Let's keep going. We have a lot more walking to do. Why, this is strange, it looks like the tunnel splits and goes left and right. I'd better look on the Trixter to see which way to go. I don't remember the tunnel having two ways to go from last night, but I only had my night vision, and I guess I didn't notice. Maptrixter shows to go through the right tunnel."

With Dr. Drake and Diego each carrying a torch, they all walked toward the right tunnel.

"These crystal walls are quite brilliant," Dr. Drake commented. "I noticed a crystal on Papaya's beak, but I wasn't sure what to make of it. Now, Sophie," he continued, "I'd like you to tell us about Tomas."

Just as he said this, something flew past all of them and Scottie let out a small scream.

"Are there bats in here?" Diego asked.

"No, I think that was Poncho and Paco," Sophie replied. "Paco, go tell Tomas that we're at the end of the tunnel and we'll soon be walking near the lake."

Paco swirled around Sophie's head and was out of sight. Poncho stayed with the group to ensure they all walked through the tunnel safely.

"Speaking of Tomas, this is a good time to tell us about him," Dr. Drake reminded Sophie.

"Okay, I guess I'll start from the beginning."

"You sound like you really don't want to tell us, Sis."

"Oh no, I do, it's just that Tomas isn't a, uh, person. You see, he's a bird, a toucan to be exact!"

"You want us to believe that you met a talking bird?" Diego asked in disbelief.

"Yes, that's what I want you to believe. And there are other different types of animals with Tomas. In fact, Diego, I'm sure you saw some of them when you were young, but was teased by your family when you would tell them what you saw in the forest."

"How did you know that?" Diego asked in a surprised voice.

"Well, I met one of those animals last night. His name is Jinx and he is amazing."

88

"Does he talk, too?" Scottie asked in a sarcastic voice before Diego could say anything.

"Yes, he talks, too," Sophie replied.

"I knew it!" Diego said in a convinced tone. "My family thought I was seeing things and that I was crazy at times. Will I be able to meet this Jinx animal?"

"Oh, yes, Diego. Jinx is looking forward to working with you."

"You mean working with us," Dr. Drake interrupted.

"There is a lot to explain," Sophie began. "But, yes, these creatures want or should I say have chosen to work with us because they need our help as much as we need theirs. You see, Tomas has convinced me that we all have a purpose here. That's why the Trixter has agreed to cooperate with me because we're all here as a team. This team spirit will help us to solve the monarch mystery."

"I think it's getting lighter in here," Scottie noticed as they continued to walk through the tunnel.

"Yes, it is getting lighter. We're almost to the end of the tunnel," Sophie replied excitedly. "Dr. Drake and Diego, why don't you put the torches in those wall crevices. We won't need them any more," she said with a smile.

CHAPTER TEN

The Crystal Canyon

Poncho now flew ahead of them to let the creatures know that Sophie and the rest were about to walk into the canyon. Just as they began to leave the tunnel, the trail they walked on was washed in sunlight and surrounded with hundreds of colorful flowers. Suddenly, Papaya came swooping toward them and landed on Dr. Drake's shoulder.

"Why, hello, Papaya. You seem to be right at home here," Dr. Drake commented as he noticed more crystals on the parrot's beak shimmering in the bright sun. His hat would come in handy, he thought as he squinted his eyes.

Sophie showed them where she walked last night, but they could barely focus on what she was saying. The sunlit canyon was making everything they looked at shimmer as if the sun was right next to them!

"This is incredible," Diego said in a loud whisper.

As they walked under a giant banyan tree, Dr. Drake could hardly focus his eyes on just one thing. There were large prehistoric-looking trees of all kinds and flowering plants everywhere. The lake was fed by a giant waterfall that glittered wherever you looked. He noticed a papaya tree and understood where his parrot flew to while they were still in the tunnel.

"It is beautiful, isn't it? I never seem to get tired of our canyon."

Everyone quickly looked toward one of the branches hovering over their heads in the banyan tree.

"Is that you, Tomas?" Sophie asked cautiously.

"Yes, my dear," Tomas answered as he hopped along the enormous branch from behind its leaves.

All of them gasped as they looked upon Tomas. His feathers were covered in crystals, which were brilliantly sparkling in the sunlight.

"Welcome, all of you to the Crystal Canyon, a place of beauty and refuge for many creatures and animals of this area."

Diego made the sign of a cross and mumbled something in Spanish. Dr. Drake and the girls stared at Tomas with their jaws dropped and mouths wide open.

Then Dr. Drake began to speak. "I'm not sure what kind of place this is. But if you intend to harm any of us, I can defend myself and this group!"

"And I will stand beside you!" Diego blurted out, getting over the shock of talking to a toucan.

"I promise you that we mean no harm to any of you.

This is not a hoax or a joke of any kind. We are in dire need of your help, Dr. Drake. Please give us a chance."

Dr. Drake felt a little more at ease, but kept looking around for other animals or creatures that might be in hiding or come out and talk!

"Sophie, I'm so glad that you came back with the rest of your group. We don't have much time to waste, so let's get this meeting started," Tomas said as he flapped his wings together.

After he did this, Sophie and the others heard rustling in the hibiscus bushes. Sophie could see a striped paw and then another one come out from behind the bush. As the rest of the large cat came into full view, they could see him in his splendor. He glittered as if jewels covered his entire body.

"Jinx!" Sophie blurted out with a smile. "You almost got caught this morning," she teased.

Scottie then realized, as Sophie had earlier, that what she had thought was a snake before wasn't a snake. It was Jinx's tail! "This is amazing," she said in an astonished voice.

"Yes, I know, I am quite unique," Jinx responded as he looked at all of them staring at him.

"This is Jinx," Tomas introduced. "He will be assisting you as you leave the canyon and continue your journey. But first, we need to talk about what is happening here in the canyon," Tomas continued. "As you can see, this is a special place, a refuge for many animals as well as insects. They come here for strength and rest before going on to their final desti-nation in Mexico or wherever their destiny may take them. We have noticed a change in the pattern of one such insect, the monarch butterfly. We have plenty of milkweed plants for them, but no butterflies have come to pollinate the plants or lay eggs before their continued migration. We think they are being threatened in some way, which makes us very concerned. This is why we've allowed you to come here and team up with us to find the monarchs."

"Have you noticed anything strange in the land surrounding the Crystal Canyon?" Dr. Drake asked, getting over the fact that he was now talking with a toucan and a large cat-like creature!

"Yes, I've noticed some human activity on the north trail beyond the lake and out of the canyon," Jinx replied.

"What kind of activity?" Diego asked as he stepped toward Jinx.

"The hummers and I have seen a group of hikers, with the leader showing them to a cliff area, and then they seem to disappear. The leader had a hat on and briefly turned once, so I couldn't tell what he looked like."

"Interesting," Dr. Drake commented while he stroked his chin with his left hand. "How do you think we can help?"

"This canyon runs for several miles and is surrounded by some very steep and uneven trails in the outer land," Jinx began. "I can show you a quicker route, instead of going back to the trail where your camp site was located, which will lead us to the outer land and then to the human activity I've described. Once we get there, we can decide how we can help each other even more."

"A short cut through the canyon does sound like the best way," Dr. Drake agreed.

"That sounds great to me!" Scottie announced. "How about Sophie and I take a dip in this wonderful lake while you all plan our next move."

"It does look refreshing," Sophie observed as she looked at the water and then to the others.

"It is refreshing. Go ahead and play in the water while Jinx and the others plan your next move," Tomas replied.

"Dr. Drake and Diego," Jinx began, "to ensure the best route through the canyon, we should review Maptrixter while the girls are in the lake."

The girls weren't sure they had bathing suits, but were delighted to find them in their backpacks right on top of their other clothes! Tomas was right. The lake water was warm and perfectly clear to swim in. The fish swirled around the girls' legs, glittering just like Jinx and Tomas. They truly understood why this lake and canyon were magical.

"All right, girls, it's time to dry off and get changed back into your hiking clothes," Dr. Drake yelled out to them as they were having a splashing contest.

Once the girls were dried and dressed and back-packs were ready to go, Jinx told the group to follow him to the outer land, using the route Maptrixter "glowed" for them. Poncho and Paco followed by flying and darting above their heads, while Papaya settled onto Dr. Drake's shoulder.

As they walked northward on the canyon trail, Scottie looked up and saw a bunch of ripe bananas on a large and tall banana tree. "Boy, swimming sure made me hungry," she whined. "Maybe if I start to jump, I'll be able to reach high enough to pick that bunch of bananas," she said with a giggle.

Sophie came walking up from behind her. "Yeah, right, Sis," she replied sarcastically.

Scottie didn't care how silly she looked. She was in such a good mood that she took off her pack and really began to jump, mostly to annoy Sophie. She looked pretty silly, jumping about 2 to 3 feet high. She decided to reach up into the air, pretending to pick the yummy fruit. She felt there was a change to her jumping. She wasn't jumping just 3 feet, she was jumping 5 feet! Then 7 feet! Then 10 feet!

Sophie ran to where Scottie was bouncing from to test the ground. It was solid as a rock and not the least bit bouncy!

"Oh, my gosh!" Sophie shouted so that everyone ahead of them turned to watch what was going on.

Scottie continued to jump higher and higher, now at 15 feet or almost a two-story building!

"Whoa!" Scottie yelled as if she were riding a horse. "I'm jumping so high, I think I can reach the bananas!"

And sure enough, Scottie was able to pull at the bunch of fruit. After the fourth try, the bananas fell to the ground.

Scottie was then able to slow herself down, jumping lower and lower. "I don't think I've ever jumped that high before. It's like I'm on a really bouncy trampoline," she said breathlessly.

"Scottie, are you alright?" Dr. Drake asked as he and Diego ran up to her.

"I'm fine," she exclaimed. "It doesn't even hurt when I land on my feet."

Diego couldn't believe it. "You must have jumped 20 feet high!"

"Scottie," Sophie began in an excited voice, "I think you've found your special talent. I wonder if you can jump from tree to tree like a flying squirrel."

"I don't know," Scottie replied with a smile, "but I'd love to find out. I know. I'll jump from the outer limbs of each tree that hangs over the lake water. That way if I fall, I'll just splash into the water instead of hitting the ground," Scottie turned to look at Dr. Drake. "Is that okay?"

Just as he nodded yes, Tomas flew to one of the trees that Scottie was going to jump onto first.

"Focus on the branch you want to jump to, Scottie, and you'll be just fine," Tomas coached reassuringly.

"Tomas," Sophie blurted out in a surprised voice, "we thought you stayed back."

"I decided to follow along until you all get to the outer canyon trail. Jinx and the hummers will then stay with you until you all return to the canyon."

Sophie smiled. She liked the thought of coming back to such a special and magical place.

Scottie looked at Tomas and hopped a few short practice jumps. She then jumped up as hard as she could while reaching up to the large rubber tree branch that Tomas was perched upon. She almost closed her eyes as she landed on her feet on top of the large branch. Quickly, she reached for another branch close to where she landed to steady herself.

Sophie yelled up to Scottie, "All right, you did it! Now do as Tomas said and concentrate on just one branch of the other tree to jump to, like you did when you were determined to reach the bananas."

Scottie studied the rubber tree and its branches. She chose one that hung over the water the farthest. Okay, you can do this, she said to herself and then counted one, two, three! She must have "flown" 15 feet to the other tree and landed on the branch standing up. She began to wobble back and forth because the branch was a little narrow where she landed.

"Quick," Diego yelled, "reach for another branch before you fall into the lake!"

Just in the nick of time, Scottie grabbed a branch with both hands. One more wobble and she would have splashed into the water.

"You did it! You did it!" Sophie shouted, jumping up and down.

Poncho and Paco began flying around Scottie as if to congratulate her.

Dr. Drake and Diego just stared at her as she stood on that tree branch.

"I've never seen anything like that," Diego said with a tone of wonder in his voice.

"Scottie, I think it's time to jump down now," Dr. Drake suggested. "We'll rest here and eat some of those great looking bananas you picked before we continue to hike on the trail."

Scottie walked along the branch to get closer to the tree trunk. She easily jumped down from there. Dr. Drake checked Scottie's ankles and knees for any sprains or pains. Scottie assured him that she was fine and ready to eat.

"So, Jinx," Dr. Drake began to ask while peeling his banana, "how much further do we need to hike before we get to the outer trail and out of the canyon?"

"We walk toward the waterfall, where the outer trail will be very close. In fact, the waterfall is how we get out!"

"Oh, how exciting," Scottie exclaimed, "another sneaky way to get out of the Crystal Canyon."

"Look!" Diego shouted as he peeled back his banana to eat it. They all looked to where he was pointing and saw three yellow monkeys taking the rest of the bunch that fell from the tree.

"Oh, those are our gecko monkeys that live here in the canyon," Jinx explained. "They've been with us all along. You just didn't notice them because they change color depending on what they are next to. They are also quiet as mice and will help us out of the canyon if we need them."

"This place is amazing," Sophie and Scottie said to each other as they took their last bites of banana.

CHAPTER ELEVEN

Professor Z

Once everyone had eaten their bananas, Tomas wished them a safe journey and was gone. They all put their backpacks on and began to hike out of the Crystal Canyon. As the group got closer to the waterfall, Jinx instructed them to walk in a single line behind him. Just as it seemed they were going to walk into the waterfall, Jinx turned sharply to the right and began to climb up what seemed to be over 50 very steep steps. The stairs formed a trail that was darkened by the shade of the overgrown trees and bushes surrounding the trail. They all followed Jinx slowly because the steps were a bit slippery as well.

Jinx could tell they were having difficulties walking up the steps. "There are vines running along side the steps. Use them to steady and to pull yourselves up the trail."

They reached down to find the vines that were hidden underneath dead leaves and other small plants. Dr. Drake and Diego pulled them up toward their waist. The girls realized the vines reminded them of a rope used to swing across a lake and drop into the water! Each man had a vine with one girl behind him. They noticed that the vines became tighter and less wobbly as they pulled themselves up the steps. Diego looked behind him and could barely believe what he saw. About 20 gecko monkeys (now the color of green leaves) were holding the ends of the vines as if to play tug-of-war. This steadied the vines while the hikers pulled themselves up the stairs.

"Well, I'll be," Dr. Drake muttered to himself as he also looked back.

"Please, keep climbing," Jinx urged as they slowly went up the stairs.

Sophie noticed that the plants around them were huge and covered the stairs in many places.

"It seems like we're climbing up steps of an ancient pyramid," Diego whispered to Dr. Drake. He nodded in agreement.

They continued to hike up and up, sometimes releasing the vines to use their hands to crawl up the steps ahead to keep themselves from tripping. Finally, they reached the top of the stepped trail, which led them to the trunk of another giant banyan tree. Jinx waited for everyone to get near him and then they all walked in single file through what seemed to be an opening in the tree's enormous trunk. As they walked through the tree, they came out into bright sunlight behind some large boulders. Jinx told them to wait while he crouched down and sprung to the left, as if to attack, and was gone. Minutes later, he returned.

"All is clear," Jinx announced as he came back into view. "Follow me and be very quiet."

Once again, they all walked in single file behind one another to get to a trail that looked like the one Dr. Drake walked on the other day after they'd set up camp.

"The human activity was this way," Jinx directed on the new trail as they hiked into thicker forest.

After walking for what seemed a long time, Dr. Drake asked Scottie to see if she could jump up to a thick limb of a pine tree just ahead of them.

"It looks about 30 feet high. Do you think you can do it?"

"That branch up there?" Scottie asked as she pointed to it. "No problem!"

"Good, then take this laser telephoto camera and put its cord around your neck. This camera will allow you to take close-up pictures of anything that might look unusual."

Everyone stopped to take off their packs and to watch Scottie.

"Okay, here I go!" Scottie squatted down really low to get better jumping speed and began to swing her arms forward and back. Then suddenly . . . whoosh! Scottie was on that large branch in seconds!

"Wow, Sis," Sophie shouted up to her, "you're getting better and better at this every time you jump."

Poncho and Paco flew up to be with Scottie.

"What do you see?" Diego hollered up to her.

"Let me steady myself and I'll start to look around and take pictures," she replied.

At first, all Scottie could see were lots and lots of trees and mountains in the distance. And then, something caught her eye. It looked like a clearing off the trail or a meadow that was near a dark gray cloud that looked like smoke.

Scottie sniffed the air, but couldn't smell anything burning. Well, that's weird, she thought and lifted up the camera to start taking pictures. She noticed some movement in the clearing of the trees, so she used the telephoto function of the camera to get a closer look. Scottie could now see that the movement was made by a group of hikers. One man, who seemed like the leader, had a hat on like Dr. Drake's, long white hair in a ponytail, and dark sunglasses. He was pointing at the others and then at some boxes.

Scottie then looked down at Dr. Drake and shouted, "I'm getting some great pictures of a group of men a few miles from here and also some shots of what looks like smoke that's near them." She raised the camera to take more pictures of the group, but they were gone. That was quick, she thought to herself.

"Dr. Drake," Sophie began, "that camera you have, I've never seen anything like it. Are Scottie and I in another year, like the future?"

"Yes, Sophie, we are in the future."

"Then why aren't we older?"

"That's another feature of the frame that is so amazing. The humans the frame allows to walk through it aren't altered in any way," he answered with a wink.

104

"I see," Sophie murmured to herself. "Oh, my gosh, that's why we didn't know that you and Auntie Jill are married because it hasn't happened yet in our time!"

"Exactly!" Dr. Drake stated with a chuckle.

"Look out below, I'm jumping down now," Scottie yelled just before she came down from the tree's branch. "I was able to get some close-up pictures of the hikers," she said as she handed the camera to Dr. Drake. "It looked like the leader was an older man with white hair in a ponytail and he wore a hat like yours."

"Well, that's interesting," Dr. Drake said as he began to look at the digital pictures.

"What is it?" Diego asked.

"It sounds like Scottie described a colleague of mine that I did some research with a long time ago. He was in charge of a huge project down in the Amazon jungle. We were trying to crack the code of how insects communicate with each other." Dr. Drake looked at the pictures and began to scowl. "Just as I suspected. It is the professor."

"Who?" both girls asked at the same time.

"It's Professor Zooger," Dr. Drake stated.

"You mean as in booger?" Scottie asked with a giggle.

Sophie saw how serious Dr. Drake looked and elbowed Scottie in her side to get her to be quiet.

"What were you saying about a code?" Diego asked.

"You've all listened to the radio, right?" Dr. Drake began. "We can listen to different radio stations by using radio waves. I like to listen to AM stations, where AM stands for amplitude modulation."

"Sophie and I listen to our favorite pop music on an FM station. What does the FM stand for?"

"It means frequency modulation. These radio waves have various band widths and are all around us," Dr. Drake answered.

"You mean we breathe radio?" Scottie interrupted in a concerned voice.

"Not exactly," Dr. Drake replied with a smile. "We just breathe air. Professor Zooger and I believed that insects not only use their antennae to direct their migration patterns but also might have their own airwave frequency, which could be controlled in some way to help them find various plants easier. We began to call this communication code, or frequency, insect modulation."

"Or IM," Sophie added.

"Yes, and we were getting very close to proving this theory when suddenly the money funded by Brazil's government and the university that sponsored the project came to an abrupt end. At least, that is what Professor Zooger told me. At first I protested, but the professor was in charge of this project so I had to agree. I always thought that it was strange how Professor Zooger seemed okay with the cancellation. Just imagine if humans were to understand this insect communication code. We'd be able to see how to work with insects for farming and other possibilities."

"You could use the insects to help grow plants in the Crystal Canyon and around the world where people are hungry," Scottie suggested.

"That's right," Dr. Drake agreed. "I've always thought that Professor Zooger wanted the IM code for himself so he could see what the insects could do for him specifically. In fact, now that I've seen his picture, I wouldn't be surprised if he has something to do with the disappearance of the monarchs!"

"Can I see the picture of him?" Sophie asked.

Dr. Drake showed her and Diego the digital photo.

"Oh, my!" Sophie gasped. "This is the man that I ran into at the hotel. Remember when our door was unlocked?"

"Yes, I remember. I thought the maid had forgotten to lock it," Dr. Drake replied.

"And," Scottie theorized, "I bet that Professor Booger, I mean Zooger, was looking for your room but had to leave quickly when we were coming up the stairs to our room."

"I think you're onto something," Dr. Drake agreed while looking at the other pictures she took. "There's something strange about this photo. Look at where Professor Zooger and his group are standing in the trail. Just beyond it, there is a cloud of dark smoke or something else in the air. Do any of you smell smoke?"

They all shook their heads no.

"Hmm, we'd better keep hiking toward that clearing to see what the professor is up to," Dr. Drake suggested as he put his backpack on.

They all agreed and began to hike on the trail toward Professor Zooger's location.

CHAPTER TWELVE

Zip It!

*A*fter they had all walked a few yards, Jinx said, "I think I'll go ahead with Poncho and Paco. I can run to that area in half the time it will take for all of you to get there. I'll also be able to scout out the area for any danger or traps."

"Great idea," Diego agreed. "I'm going to run ahead too. Jinx can then show me where Professor Zooger and his men were last seen. I know I can't run as fast as Jinx, but I've always been a sprinter in school, so I'll make good time."

Dr. Drake took Diego's backpack and they all wished him luck as he left with Jinx and the hummers.

"That clearing looks about three miles from here," Scottie estimated based on her experience at the ranch when she and Sophie would ride their horses. Gosh, she thought, I wish Starburst were here now. I could ride to the clearing much faster than I can walk.

They all checked their canteens to make sure they had plenty of water and began to hike the next three miles or so.

As Jinx ran on the trail, he picked up the scent of the men that Scottie had seen from the tree limb. He left broken twigs on the trail so that Diego and the rest of the group would be sure to stay on the same trail. When Jinx got to the clearing, their scent still lingered, but no humans were in sight. He told the hummers to fly around in the area, but they didn't see any humans either.

"Why, Diego, I am impressed!" Jinx exclaimed as Diego came into the clearing. "You are a fast runner after all."

Diego gave Jinx a slight nod as he leaned over to put his hands on his knees and catch his breath. He then began to walk around the clearing and off the trail to a wooded area, which led him to a ravine.

"Hey, Jinx," Diego shouted, "I think I've found something. This is why those men seemed to disappear." Diego pointed to something among the trees that started at the edge of the ravine. "This is the fastest way to cross this ravine. It's a zip line!"

Just then Dr. Drake and the girls walked up to Diego.

"We could hear you shouting for Jinx," Sophie said breathlessly. "What's a zip line?"

As she asked, Dr. Drake was inspecting the harness attached to the thick woven wire cable.

"As you can see," Dr. Drake began to explain, "you sit in the harness attached to this pulley system, which allows you to zip along the cable at a rather high speed to get to the other end of the cable. The rider stops the harness by pulling this lever, which makes the wheels slowly stop the harness on the cable. Professor Zooger was very clever to put this zip line here. It looks like it goes down to the ravine floor."

"I'll go first!" Diego blurted out in a courageous voice.

"First, we'll put a pack in the harness to see if it can carry the load of the backpack. If it stays intact, then you can go first, Diego," Dr. Drake replied.

"Well, I'm not waiting for that," Jinx observed. "I'll take this trail and see you at the end of the zip line. It looks like it will take some time, even with my speed. Poncho and Paco, go with Diego when he's ready," Jinx ordered.

Jinx left before anyone could reply. The hummers began to dart around Diego's head in anticipation of his ride on the zip line. Diego put his backpack in the harness and also found some rocks to put in the pack.

"These rocks will weigh down my pack even more to make sure the pulley system and harness can carry my body without snapping off the wire," Diego explained.

Everyone nodded in agreement as Diego secured the pack into the harness seat.

"How will you know when the pack has reached the other end of the cable?" Scottie asked.

"I'm going to keep my hand on the cable. When it no longer vibrates, I'll know that the pulley system and harness are no longer sliding," Diego answered.

"Notice the upper cable that runs above this cable you zip on. It loops from the lower cable to these pulleys attached to those trees. Once the pack is at the other end, we'll start pulling the lower cable and the pack toward us and the entire upper cable will also move. First, though, I need to release this clamp. This clamp, I noticed, keeps the cable from moving when someone wants to zip on it."

"I knew I picked the right guide to accompany us on this journey. Good job, Diego!" Dr. Drake commented as Diego began to push the harness away from them to gain speed and zip along the cable. Soon the backpack was out of sight.

Only minutes had passed, but it seemed much longer when Diego looked at the others with a smile and said, "I think the pack has reached the other side. I don't feel any more vibrations."

Everyone felt the cable and sure enough, it was very still and cold to the touch.

"All right everyone, help me pull the lower cable toward us to see if the harness and the pack come back in one piece," Diego instructed. "The cable didn't snap, so the weight of the pack also seems to be okay."

They all began pulling, when Sophie called out to everyone, "Look!" They could see the harness dangling on the cable about 15 feet from where they stood. The backpack was still in the harness seat, too.

"Hooray," both girls shouted.

"Let's hurry so I can get started," Diego announced excitedly. He pulled his pack out of the harness and put it on after taking out all of the rocks. Just before he got into the harness, both girls ran up to hug him and Dr. Drake walked up to shake his hand.

"Good luck, Diego," he said and then stepped back to give Diego room to run and step off the edge of the ravine. The hummers were very excited and began to dart all around Diego. Dr. Drake could tell that Papaya wanted to join Poncho and Paco, so he stroked her neck and back feathers to keep her calm and on his shoulder. "You can fly when the girls take their turn on the zip line," he assured her.

"I'll send the hummers back to you when I reach the other side. That way, you'll know to begin to pull the cable so the harness will come back to you. Poncho and Paco will also be a sign that I'm all right."

Diego crossed himself and said a short prayer. "Uno, dos, tres," Diego shouted and then, whoosh, he began speeding along the cable. He held on tightly as the pulley system whined a high pitch sound as the harness zipped along. Diego noticed that the ravine had a variety of plants and trees. He also saw a grove of coconut trees in the distance, close to where the gray cloud was.

Suddenly, Diego had to turn quickly to avoid a tree branch that was reaching out near the cable. He started to spin round and round as he continued to zip along.

"Whoa!" Diego yelled out and finally steadied himself. He soon realized that the pulley system began to slow down as the cable began to get thicker, as at the other end where he started. He began to pull the lever to stop the harness and within seconds, Diego stopped at the end of the zip line over a ledge jetting out from the ravine wall.

That Professor Zooger sure is clever, Diego thought. As his feet touched down on the ledge, Diego got his balance and looked down. He was at least 20 feet up from the ground, but he spotted a rope ladder that led to the ravine floor.

"Ah, ha!" Diego shouted to himself and quickly began to get out of the harness. Before he sent the hummers back, he wrote a note to the group and attached it to the harness, warning them of the tree limb and telling them to be sure to balance themselves in the harness or they might spin like a toy top!

"There," he said to the hummers. With the note secured to the harness clip, he ordered the hummers to fly back to Dr. Drake and the girls. Diego also began to push the cable after releasing the cable clamp that had stopped it from moving. This way, Dr. Drake and the girls would notice the cable moving toward them, also signaling that Diego was out of the harness and ready for the next person to zip. Now for the ladder, he thought.

As Diego began to climb down the ladder, he realized that he'd never seen this ravine before. It was rocky with all sorts of plants and trees. He started to walk along a trail that began from the ladder. Diego gasped as he looked up at the trees. He saw the smoke or gray cloud that Dr. Drake commented on earlier, except this smoke didn't smell and was moving in many different ways. In fact, it wasn't smoke or a cloud at all. It was thousands of dragonflies!

The bugs flew up and over the trail that seemed to lead to nowhere. After watching the dragonflies for a few minutes, he continued to walk on the rocky trail. Diego thought he heard something but decided it was nothing. No, he did hear something, a deep low growling sound. Diego stopped and turned around very slowly.

What he saw was the biggest dog he'd ever seen, like a large wolf or even bigger, following him! It began to show its fangs as it growled, drool dripping from its lower jaw as it walked closer to Diego. He realized that he needed to get away as fast as possible.

Suddenly, Diego turned and began to sprint as fast as he could on the trail. He could hear the dog getting closer to him. As he braced himself for the attack, he heard a strange sound from behind him. While still running, Diego turned and from the corner of his eye saw a massive object that seemed to fly past him and tackle the dog.

As Diego stopped running, he saw something roll over and over with the giant dog. He then realized that the object was Jinx! With his tiger stripes and thick tail, Jinx looked like he'd doubled in size. Every striped inch of fur on his back was standing straight up, still glistening even in the shade of the trees and dragonflies. Once Jinx stopped rolling with the part wolf animal, Diego could see that Jinx was on top of it. The dog looked terrified as Jinx's fangs were about to bite down around its furry neck. Diego gasped loudly, which made Jinx hesitate and look up at Diego. The dog saw this as an opportunity to get away. Its powerful back legs pushed Jinx off and the giant dog was free. Instantly, it began to sprint away into the bushes, yelping the entire time it was running away.

Jinx stood up as straight as possible. He shook his whole body as if to get the giant dog's scent off of him and then turned to walk toward an amazed Diego.

"W-wow Jinx," Diego stuttered, "w-what took you so long to get here?" Diego then laughed nervously as Jinx gave him a sarcastic look, rolling his big brown eyes.

"We'd better see if the others have arrived before we explore any further," Jinx ordered as he began to walk back to the zip line and the ledge. Diego nodded and followed Jinx without another word.

CHAPTER THIRTEEN

So We Meet Again!

Scottie kept her hand on the cable to feel the vibration from Diego's zip line ride. Soon the cable was still. "I think Diego is at the other end now," Scottie called out to Sophie and Dr. Drake. "I don't feel any vibration on the cable."

"We need to wait until the hummers fly back before we begin to pull the lower cable toward us," Dr. Drake replied.

After what seemed like forever to Scottie and Sophie, the cable began to move toward them from Diego pushing the cable at his end. They noticed that the cable clamp was sprung loose by a connected rope that ran from Diego's end of the zip line all the way to their side of the zip line. Professor Zooger certainly thought of everything,

Dr. Drake thought to himself. Soon, Poncho and Paco were buzzing Scottie's head as they pulled the cable toward them.

"As soon as we see the harness," Dr. Drake began, "you two need to decide who will go next. Papaya will follow you, and I will zip last after she flies back to let me know you two are safely on the other side."

"Look!" Sophie blurted out. "I see the harness and there's a note attached to it."

Sophie took the note off the harness when it got close enough to grab it. They all agreed that Diego's zip line tips would be helpful.

"I'll go first," Sophie volunteered.

"I wish I could just jump to the other side," Scottie said while observing how wide the ravine was. "Okay, Sis, you go first, but be very careful."

"I will, Scottie. Okay, Dr. Drake, help me put on this harness and I'll be at the other side of the ravine in no time."

Scottie helped put Sophie's pack on her lap, making sure Maptrixter was securely inside. She then gave Sophie a hug. Dr. Drake gave her a hug for good luck, too, and allowed Papaya to perch on her shoulder, signaling that she could follow Sophie to the other end of the zip line. He then gave her a big push, and she was off with Papaya and the hummers!

"Be sure to send Papaya back to us when you reach the other side," Dr. Drake called out to remind Sophie as she zipped out of sight.

Zipping along, Sophie felt like a bird flying through the trees. She could see the tree branch that Diego warned them about in the note and was very careful not to hit it. Sophie also kept her legs out in front of her to steady herself and to keep from spinning. Papaya and the hummingbirds flew next to her the entire time. When she could see the ledge at the end of the cable, the pulley system began to slow down.

Sophie now could look around a bit and noticed the moving gray cloud. That's not smoke, she said to herself. Oooh, yuck, I think it's a bunch of bugs! She looked closer and realized they were dragonflies, and the insects were flying everywhere! She soon was at the ravine ledge and used her feet to guide herself onto it as Diego had done. After she felt stable standing up, she began to get out of the harness.

"Okay, Papaya, fly back to Scottie and Dr. Drake to let them know it's Scottie's turn to zip!" Papaya rested on her shoulder and cocked her head in a way that let Sophie know that she understood and was soon in the air, flying back to Dr. Drake. The hummers stayed with Sophie to keep her company.

"Now, I wonder where Diego went," Sophie said to Poncho and Paco as she looked around on the ledge. She soon noticed the rope ladder that led to the ravine floor, but decided it would be best to wait for the others. Besides, all of those dragonflies gave her the creeps and she needed to start pushing the cable back up to Scottie.

Diego and Jinx didn't say much while they walked back to the end of the zip line and the ledge. Diego could see the girls waiting for Dr.

Drake to step out of the harness. Diego waved to them and they waved back.

"Hello, everyone," Diego shouted up to them, "I hope you had a nice trip!"

They all laughed and began to climb down the ladder.

"Diego," Dr. Drake began, "we thought we heard a dog yelping. Is everything all right?"

"It is now," Diego replied in a factual tone.

"It looks like we should walk this way along the trail," Dr. Drake suggested as he looked up at the dragonflies.

"Why are there so many of them flying around here?" Scottie asked Dr. Drake as if she tasted something sour.

"They must be attracted to something that's in this area. Dragonflies will eat other insects. In fact, they attack their unsuspecting prey from below," Dr. Drake explained.

Suddenly, they all looked at each other at the same time and blurted "butterflies!"

"I have a feeling that there is a connection between the dragonflies and the location of the missing monarchs," Dr. Drake continued. "In fact, what do we have here?"

The trail had ended into what seemed to be a wall of vines.

"Wait! I see something moving behind these vines," Sophie observed as her eyes adjusted while looking through the vines. She could now see in the darkness beyond the vines. There were two wrought iron doors that filled the entire area behind the wall of vines. The doors had bars and a fine metal mesh attached to the bars.

"Oh, wow!" Sophie gasped. "It looks like this is a huge cave and it's full of something on the other side of these doors. Let me focus a little more . . . we found them, we found them!" Sophie shouted.

"How can Sophie see anything? It's so dark," Diego wondered out loud.

"We found out back at the hotel that Sophie has an unusual ability to see in the dark. Her eyes know when to adjust and she can see as well in the dark as in the daylight," Dr. Drake answered.

"It's like my new talent," Scottie explained, "except instead of jumping super high, Sophie can see when it's pitch black around her."

"You two sure are full of surprises!" Diego said with a smile.

"Okay, Sis, what did we find?" Scottie asked as she ran up next to her.

"The monarch butterflies are in the cave! It looks like there are a million of them," Sophie described in wonder. Just as Sophie said that, a butterfly managed to escape from the door hinges. As the monarch floated away, a dragonfly immediately attacked it. As the group watched the helpless butterfly, none of them noticed that a loud noise broke the silence just above them. Instantly, a large net made out of rope, possibly used for fishing, was hurled down upon them!

Several men dressed in black seemed to come out of nowhere to hold the net down. Scottie and Sophie were about to scream, but Diego hugged them and told them to stay calm before any noise came out. A small gate within one side of the huge iron doors began to open.

"Well, well, if it isn't Dr. Drake. So we meet again. I thought I'd gotten you off my trail long ago back in Brazil," the gray-haired man said in a gruff voice.

"Professor Zooger, I should have known you were the cause of the missing monarchs! These insects can't hurt a thing. Why on earth are you keeping them?"

"Oh, no, Dr. Drake, this is only temporary. I'm not keeping them for me. In fact, I'm in negotiations with, let's say, the highest bidding nation. You see, I've discovered that farmers really love these monarchs, almost as much as they love bees. But we all know that bees can't pollinate all the world's crops, now can they?" Professor Z. explained with a smile. He then yelled at the men. "Guards, take Dr. Drake and his, uh, guests through the gate and put them into the pit so I can decide what to do with them." He then stepped through the gate and disappeared.

As Professor Zooger's guards let the group stand up with the net still covering them, Scottie whispered to Diego, "Where did Jinx and Papaya go?"

He and the others looked around and then Sophie spotted Jinx's thick striped tail just barely noticeable next to a tree. They could also hear Papaya squawking on a branch nearby. Sophie slightly elbowed Dr. Drake, who looked at her and then toward where her eyes were looking at Jinx's tail.

Dr. Drake nodded just as the net was lifted off of them. All of them were quickly shuttled through the smaller iron gate and through at least 50 chains hanging just inside the doorway to prevent any butterflies from escaping. Sophie could instantly see that the cave must be as tall as a five-story building and as wide as at least two houses. She gasped also when she saw millions of butterflies everywhere her eye could see. Sophie could tell that they were resting on thousands of chains hung from the cave ceiling. Other butterflies were flying to land on various nectar and fruit trays that were placed throughout the cave.

"This cave must go on for miles," Dr. Drake observed in amazement as his eyes adjusted to the dim light.

"Why, yes it does," Professor Zooger answered as he stepped out of the shadows and onto a platform about 10 feet above them. "This magnificent cave is compliments of an ancient civilization that lived here hundreds of years ago. I've completely explored this cave and its many passage ways and realized that this would be the perfect place to hold my beautiful butterflies. And this cave is where the monarchs will stay until I sell them to the highest bidding country. I can barely believe how brilliant I am," the professor said with a crooked smile.

"So you figured out the IM code of the monarchs," Dr. Drake stated loudly.

"Oh, yes, and with the code, I've been able to control the butterflies' migration pattern. You remember Satellite 3-5-9 and its signal path," Professor Zooger continued without Dr. Drake's reply. "Well, I was able to combine that coordinate with the IM code and, voilà, I noticed that I could control the flight pattern of the monarch butterfly. With this knowledge, I didn't need you anymore snooping around in the Amazon research camp. So I conveniently cancelled the insect project. Oh, and speaking of insects, don't you just love my insect guards out there among the trees? I release a few butterflies every now and then to keep the dragonflies interested in what's in the cave. Yes, I'm amazingly clever," Professor Zooger continued to brag, "and I can see that you all have been clever yourselves. I'm not sure what scared Macro away, but I'll make sure my guards are doubled at the front of these gates in case there are any more surprises."

Professor Zooger then pointed to an area of the cave. "As you can see, there is a large pit near where you all are standing. The ancient people used this pit for various sacrifices to their gods. Of course, I won't be doing that to you, at the moment anyway. So please use the rope ladder to lower yourselves into the pit," he ordered.

Diego began to resist.

"I wouldn't do anything stupid if I were you. It would be a shame for any of you to fall 15 feet into the pit and possibly break your neck," Professor Zooger sneeringly shouted.

Dr. Drake nodded for them to climb the ladder down into the pit. The guards took Dr. Drake's and Diego's packs before they climbed down. There were a few torches lit to help them see the pit floor. It was bare except for a large log to sit on.

"I put some snacks in your pack, Sophie," Diego began to say. "We might as well eat something while we figure out what to do next."

"Good idea," Dr. Drake agreed. "Eventually, Zooger's guards will quit giving us so much attention and then I hope we can figure out how to get out of this pit."

"I know we'll get out because Jinx and Papaya will bring help," Sophie stated with assurance.

They all nodded and began to nibble at their food.

CHAPTER FOURTEEN

To the Rescue!

Jinx made sure that Sophie would see his tail, moving it just slightly to let her and the rest know he was safe and would be back with help. Once his signal was understood, Jinx leaped away from the tree and sprinted back to the Crystal Canyon. Papaya and the hummingbirds flew just above him the entire way. As they entered the canyon, Papaya flew ahead of Jinx to find Tomas.

"Jinx, get a drink of water and tell me what happened and where the children are," Tomas ordered urgently.

Jinx told Tomas everything. They both agreed that Jinx and Papaya needed help rescuing the girls, Dr. Drake, and Diego. They stood there on the trail, both pacing in opposite directions and back to one another. Each would begin to suggest something and would stop, realizing the idea wouldn't work. Jinx looked on the ground and noticed a banana that was left behind earlier by the gecko monkeys. He picked it up with his teeth and ran over to Tomas.

"Oh, no thank you, Jinx, I'm not . . .," Tomas' round eyes got very large. "Why didn't I think of that? Why yes, that's perfect. Hurry, Jinx, take Papaya and go!"

Jinx took off from the trail and ran into the jungle area of the canyon. Now which direction should I go to next? Ah, there is the narrow tree trunk bridge, Jinx thought to himself.

"Papaya, go find the clearing and let me know which way to go after I cross this bridge," Jinx ordered as he crossed. He found some shade to wait in and began to think about how he was going to ask for help. Papaya flew back within minutes, circled Jinx, and flew off. Jinx quickly jumped to his paws and ran toward where Papaya was flying, heading for the clearing.

As Jinx entered the jungle clearing, he heard some rustling in the far banyan tree. Jinx barely noticed the monkey. In fact, he knew from seeing him in other parts of the canyon that he wasn't much different from the others, but he had a gift that the others didn't have. Chewy had an amazing ability to find food. This ability made him the leader of the gecko monkeys. Jinx could see what looked like a floating twig moving upward, just below two glowing black eyes, to a mouth full of big square teeth. Yes, Jinx thought, this is Chewy all right.

Chewy sat lazily in the crook of the giant banyan tree chewing on a twig, similar to how humans chew on a toothpick. He was barely visible because his skin and hair

128

can change and turn the exact color or pattern of what he is next to. In this instance, Chewy looked like the bark of the banyan tree.

"WhyJinx,whatbringsyouheretomyhome?"

"And, hello to you, too, Chewy," Jinx shouted up to him. "Could you please talk slower so I can understand you better?"

"OhIamsorry," Chewy cleared his throat. "I said, what brings you here to my home?"

"I thought that's what you said. I just can't get used to your speed-talk language," Jinx answered. "I'm here to ask you and your clan for help. Do you remember the humans who were here earlier today?"

"Of course, they had a hard time climbing out of the canyon, so we helped them. In fact, we've been near them the entire time they arrived in the Crystal Canyon, but once again, they didn't notice us," Chewy said with a smile. "We sure enjoyed the delicious bananas they left behind, too!"

"Yes, well, after your clan helped them out of the canyon, my journey with them took us to an enormous cave. Within the cave, to our amazement, was the entire colony of the beautiful monarch butterflies."

"Why are they in this cave?" Chewy asked as he sat up in the tree.

"They are in the cave because the butterflies have been captured and I'm not sure why. What I am sure of is that the humans you helped have also been captured and are now in extreme danger."

"Then something must be done!" Chewy stood up and threw away his twig.

"You're right, something must be done, and Tomas and I agree that the gecko monkeys are our only hope to save the monarchs and the humans," Jinx said as if he were cheering. "The children were guided here by Maptrixter," Jinx continued. "The children then guided Dr. Drake and Diego to this canyon. They were all meant to help the monarchs and now we are meant to help them."

"Yes, my clan and I have watched Diego grow from a small boy to a young man. He is a good man, so we will help you," Chewy replied.

"Excellent!" Jinx shouted. "I'll tell you about the cave when you come down from the tree so we can head out of the canyon and toward the ravine."

Chewy began to move his arms up and down to signal other monkeys that they were going to travel out of the canyon. The clan began to speed-talk and dance around Chewy and Jinx. Chewy was able to quiet them down so Jinx could tell them his plan.

"There are many guards, human guards, outside the cave entrance. Half of your clan should distract them in some way to scare them away. I've noticed huge trees are all around the cave. The other half of your monkey clan should climb up those trees and find another way into the cave from above."

The gecko monkey clan looked at Chewy for agreement. "That plan is good. We will go now!"

"One more thing," Jinx shouted before they began to leave the clearing. As we get close to the cave, there will be a humming noise and you will see what looks like smoke."

"Smoke!" a gecko monkey shouted with concern.

"Don't worry," Jinx quickly shouted back to the clan. "It's not a fire, but a huge swarm of dragonflies."

"Didyousaydragonflies?" Chewy blurted out in an excited voice.

"Yes, they are waiting to attack the monarchs that may escape the cave."

"Dragonflies are a delicacy to gecko monkeys," Chewy explained. Just then, the clan began to dance around excitedly.

"Lead the way, Jinx. We're ready to go," Chewy shouted and jumped up onto the banyan tree while the other monkeys did the same.

Jinx ran out of the clearing into the jungle, with Papaya flying and squawking over his head. All of the gecko monkeys, hundreds of them, began to swing from limb to limb and tree to tree. Their long arms changed color as they moved through the jungle toward the outer trail of the Crystal Canyon.

CHAPTER FIFTEEN

Escape and Flutter By!

Professor Zooger's guards lit a few torches to keep some light in the dark and damp cave. It wasn't very cold in the cave or in the pit, much to the girls' relief as they began to figure out their next plan of action with Dr. Drake and Diego.

"Hey, look," Sophie said in a low voice to the others. They turned to see what she was pointing at on the ground and noticed a faint light shining from her backpack. Sophie carefully opened it and realized the glow was coming from Maptrixter. They all gathered around the map to hide its light from the guards. Sophie unrolled the map and they began to study it.

They were shocked to see that Maptrixter had completely changed. In fact, the map was now of the cave and its complete inner pathways.

"Why, it's showing us different escape routes in the cave," Diego pointed out excitedly. "Look, there is the ledge that Professor Zooger stood on. Maptrixter shows how he gets to it from that inner stepped trail leading up to the top of the cave's ceiling. You can also see that there is another way off the ledge that has a stairway leading to the cave floor."

"And where is this upper opening?" Scottie asked, looking at Maptrixter and then up toward the cave ceiling.

Sophie could see perfectly in the cave and looked toward the ceiling. "It's up there," she answered while pointing above their heads. "There's hardly any light, but I can see where the sun is barely shining through an opening. It looks like it's covered with the same steel mesh as the giant wrought iron doors. I can see a handle on the frame of the cover and I can also see the steps that lead up to the cover. It looks like this cover is a mini door so someone can enter the cave from above," Sophie observed.

"If I could only jump out of here, I'd lower the rope ladder and get us out of this darned pit," Scottie said with a scowl.

"Or, you could get us into a lot more trouble," Sophie interrupted.

"Let me just see how high I can jump. Be a lookout for me, Sophie," Scottie ordered.

Just as she was about to jump, Diego rushed over and pushed down on her shoulders. "Be still. Here comes a guard. I can see the light from his flashlight coming toward the pit."

The guard's light flooded the pit for a few seconds. Diego and the rest could hear the guard mumble a few words to another guard and laugh. They then walked away and the pit was once again in dimmed, shadowy light.

When the flashlight beam was on them, Scottie noticed something strange poking out the side of Sophie's pack. She walked over and felt it. There seemed to be a large square object about six inches in her pack!

"Sophie, you might want to come over here," Scottie suggested in a hushed but puzzled voice.

Sophie walked toward her. "What's the matter?"

"I can feel something very strange in your pack. I know that Diego was just in it to get us some snacks, but let's open it and see what this object is."

"Okay, but look," Sophie answered, "I can see something bulky in your backpack, too!"

"Dr. Drake, Diego!" both girls called out at the same time.

"Come over here, quick. I think our packs are growing something!" Sophie almost shouted.

The men walked over as Scottie opened her backpack and looked inside.

"Oh, wow!" Scottie exclaimed as she reached in and pulled out her beaded rain box.

"It's beautiful," Diego commented.

"It's also growing!" Sophie added.

"Quick," Scottie blurted out while looking at Sophie, "open your pack to see what's inside."

Sure enough, Sophie reached in and pulled out her growing rain box too. "This is so weird," she said while looking at her box more closely. "Even

135

though it's bigger, my rain box looks the same as when it was smaller."

Each girl opened her own box, but couldn't hear the sound of a beating drum as they did at home. They then shrugged and closed their boxes.

"Wait!" Diego blurted out and looked around for the guards. "When you opened the boxes, something began to happen. I'm not sure what, but I think it affected the butterflies."

"Can you see anything, Sophie?" Dr. Drake asked. "In fact, open your boxes again girls and let me know, Sophie, if you can see anything unusual with the insects."

Both girls opened their rain boxes. Sophie walked to one side of the pit to see the hanging chains with the butterflies on them, while Scottie instinctively began to jump to try to see the butterflies, too.

"There must be something strange in this dirt," Scottie observed. "I can only jump about 5 feet high."

"Dr. Drake," Sophie shouted excitedly, "the boxes are doing something to the butterflies. They're leaving their chains and feeders and are flying all over the cave!"

"Hmm," Dr. Drake contemplated, "I wonder if the rain boxes are emitting some type of sound or signal, like a dog whistle that we can't hear but affects the butterflies."

"You'd better close the boxes before Professor Zooger gets suspicious," Diego suggested.

The girls closed the boxes and put them carefully back into their own packs. As the monarchs began to settle back onto the hanging chains, Sophie looked around the cave and kept focusing, for some reason, up toward the mini door in the cave ceiling. She thought she saw something move on the mesh part of the door. Sophie tapped Dr. Drake on the shoulder and pointed up toward the ceiling.

"I think there is something on the mesh of the mini door," Sophie whispered.

"Like what?"

Sophie then gasped as she kept looking at the mini door. She saw long, skinny fingers reaching through the squares in the steel mesh. There must've been 40 of them reaching through! Then all at once, the mini door began to move, inch by inch, being pulled up until the door was completely open. Sophie nudged Scottie with her elbow and pointed upward. Diego looked up too.

"It's the gecko monkeys," Sophie said in an excited whisper. "I can see them climbing down one of the chains that the butterflies didn't fly back to."

The others could now see the monkeys in the very dim light. Just then, they all heard yelling near the huge iron doors.

"Hey, hey, what's going on out there?" a guard yelled through the iron door.

"I don't know, Sergeant," was the shouted reply. "It looks like we're being attacked with coconuts! Ouch! We can't tell where they're coming from. It's, it's as if they're floating in the air and then hurling toward us!"

"Incoming!" another guard yelled to warn the others. "It's the ancient tribe's ghosts who used to live here. I told you, Sergeant, that this place was haunted," the guard continued to shout.

"I'm out of here," another guard shouted.

"Me, too, before I get hit in the head and get myself killed," yelled another guard.

As the sergeant started yelling at the guards to stay at their assigned post while he unlocked the smaller iron gate to get out of the cave, everyone could hear an ear-deafening roaring sound. Dr. Drake and everyone in the pit stood frozen and looked at one another.

"That must be Jinx and more gecko monkeys," Diego proclaimed.

Just then, the rope ladder dropped into the pit and three monkeys quickly climbed down.

"Youallmustescapenow!" It was Chewy who was commanding them to climb up the ladder.

"Quick, Sis, get your pack!" Sophie shouted to Scottie as they climbed up the ladder.

"Thiswaythisway!" Chewy ordered, pointing to the smaller gate of the iron doors.

"Wait," Scottie shouted, "the butterflies need to escape, too!"

"Dr. Drake, where is your rope?" Scottie asked.

"It's in my backpack over there." He ran over to where the guards put his and Diego's pack. Dr. Drake reached into it, pulled out the coiled rope, and threw it to Scottie.

"Dr. Drake," Diego shouted, "you go with Scottie and Sophie while I go with the monkeys to check out what is going on outside these doors."

As Diego walked through the small gate within the massive iron doors, he instantly saw Jinx and the hummers next to the sergeant. It looked as if the guard got hit quite hard with a few coconuts. "Hello, Jinx," Diego said with a smile. "Nice shot, I must say."

"Yes, the timing was perfect. After I let out my roar,

this guard froze in his boots, making him a perfect target for the monkeys," Jinx replied. "Where are the others? Are they all right?"

"Yes, thanks to you, Papaya, and the gecko monkeys, they should be out as soon as these massive doors are opened. We had better stand watch in case the other guards come back. I haven't seen Professor Zooger either, so we'd better look very carefully for any movement out in the trees that isn't a monkey," Diego suggested as he looked at the sleeping guard. "I think I'll tie this guy up with some twine so when he wakes up, he won't bother anyone!"

"Good idea, good idea!" Papaya chanted in the tree overhead, to Diego and Jinx's surprise.

Meanwhile, Scottie was looking up at the top of the iron doors where the two sides closed together.

"See that lever way up there, about 3 feet above the doors. I've noticed there is a chain that goes from the lever to some gears on the left side of the door hinges. I've also noticed that the bars on these gates are too smooth for the monkeys to climb up and reach the lever to pull it down. I think it has something to do with opening these massive iron doors," Scottie described to Sophie and Dr. Drake.

"Do you think you can jump up and pull down the lever, Sis?"

"No, I don't because there is something in this dirt that won't allow me to jump very high. But I was thinking if I use this rope to lasso the lever, then we can all pull on the rope to make the lever point down. I think this will make the chain and gears move and that will open these doors."

"Great idea, Sis!" Sophie shouted and Dr. Drake agreed.

Scottie raised her arm over her head and began to swing the rope in a circular motion, as she did when she practiced roping at the ranch. Round and round the rope loop circled over her head. She really focused on the lever and without realizing it, Scottie jumped while she released the rope from her hand. She lassoed that lever on her first try!

"That jumping sure comes in handy," Scottie exclaimed with a smile.

"Great job," they all cheered.

Scottie quickly began to tighten the loop of the rope around the lever, while Dr. Drake, Sophie, and some of the gecko monkeys began to pull on the rope. Slowly, the lever began to move downward.

"Stop!" Dr. Drake commanded. "The rope is beginning to fray and all of our pulling might snap the rope."

"Wewillclimbupthe, I mean, we will climb up the tightened rope and push down on the lever," Chewy suggested to Dr. Drake.

"That sounds like our only hope," Dr. Drake agreed.

Just then, Diego came walking in through the smaller iron gate. Dr. Drake motioned for him to come over and help with holding the rope while a few of the monkeys climbed it to reach the lever.

"Girls, while Diego and I hold the tightened rope, get those rain boxes out of your backpacks and open them up," Dr. Drake ordered. "I think the box sounds are breaking up the IM waves and in some way are messing up how Professor Zooger controls the monarch's migration signals."

Scottie and Sophie quickly ran over to their packs and struggled to pull the rain boxes out of each one. They could see the boxes growing larger and larger before their very eyes! They set the boxes on the ground and opened the lids. The moon's rays were coming through the huge iron doors and beginning to light up the cave opening. The boxes seemed to sparkle, and everyone could now hear the chanting and drumbeat sounds coming from them. At first the sounds were very low, but slowly they got louder and louder. All of the butterflies released themselves from the hanging chains and flew in what looked like a giant tornado full of color within the cave. This butterfly tornado made the chains move back and forth until they were hitting each other, filling the cave with what sounded like rain!

Chewy and the other monkeys were now at the lever. As they pushed down, the men also pulled on the rope. This time the lever crashed down with a loud thump! The lever had released the chain. This chain then released the gears that were next to the gate hinges. Round and round the gears turned, creaking and screeching as they moved. Slowly, the doors began to swing outward.

"They're moving, they're moving," both girls shouted excitedly.

"And just in time," Diego observed. "Look behind us."

They all turned to see millions of butterflies circling closer to them. As the gates opened wider and wider, the monarchs flew past them and began to pour out of the cave. The moon's rays allowed everyone to see them perfectly. The gecko monkeys could be seen swinging in the trees, gorging on dragonflies as the insects attempted to attack the butterflies. Poncho and Paco were constantly darting up and down in the air as they flew, trying to protect the butterflies as they escaped.

"No, no, no! Not my beauties!" Professor Zooger yelled.

Dr. Drake and Diego quickly turned to see him on the cave ledge. In one hand he held a large black book and in the other hand a butterfly net. He was reaching out, trying to catch the monarchs as they flew by. Professor Zooger never saw Chewy coming as he reached for the butterflies. The monkey quietly ran up the stairs that led up to the ledge. Faster than you can throw a coconut, he snatched the black book out of the professor's hands and ran back to the giant iron doors.

"Oh no, not the IM code formula," the professor screamed. "I'm ruined!" he shouted as he dropped the net and ran up the steps to the mini cave door in the ceiling. Diego quickly ran after him, but it was too late. Professor Zooger was gone.

"This is incredible," Scottie shouted to Sophie because the rain boxes were really loud now.

Suddenly, Jinx ran up to the girls and almost tackled them with delight.

"Oh, Jinx, you did it, you rescued us!" Sophie shouted as she and Scottie hugged Jinx around the neck.

"I also had help from this little one."

Just as Jinx said that, Papaya came swooping down and landed on Dr. Drake's shoulder.

"Papaya," Dr. Drake exclaimed with a smile and stroked her feathers.

Jinx looked at all of them with relief. "Dr. Drake, I want you to meet Chewy, the leader of the gecko monkeys. Without them, I would've had a hard time rescuing all of you."

"Very nice to meet you, Chewy. We thank you and your clan for taking this risk to save us from the wicked Professor Zooger."

"It's our pleasure. I believe this book belongs to you," Chewy said as he handed the IM code book to Dr. Drake.

Jinx then looked around to make sure everyone was there. "We must hurry. Chewy and his clan want to get back before daylight. They will continue to be our guides back to the Crystal Canyon."

"They're beautiful," Sophie observed while watching them in the trees. The monkeys were glowing from the moonlight's rays cast upon them, first being dark as night in the shadows and then glowing again. The butterflies were glistening, too, as they flew in the moonlight, out of the cave, and to their freedom.

Dr. Drake noticed the guard who was tied up was still out cold. He took any weapon and electronic devices from him and then untied him. "I don't think he'll be doing much harm to anyone now."

Diego and the girls agreed. They all put their backpacks on and hiked back to the canyon with a sense of relief, knowing that each of them and the monarch butterflies were now safe and free.

CHAPTER SIXTEEN

Home, Sweet Home

The Crystal Canyon valley was a welcoming sight for Sophie, Scottie, and the others. Diego knew that the girls were exhausted, so he set up their tent as the girls greeted Tomas. He told them to go to bed and he'd hear their story in the morning. Sophie and Scottie nodded and yawned at the same time, walking into their tent and both falling asleep instantly.

Scottie and Sophie slept in their tent as the sun rose brightly in the late morning sky. They both began to stir and opened their eyes at the same exact time, lying in their sleeping bags and looking at each other.

"I can't believe everything that happened yesterday," Sophie said while yawning.

"I know. It's as though we were living in an action

movie or something," Scottie blurted out as she sat up, still in her clothes from yesterday.

"It's amazing to think that we saved thousands of monarch butterflies and their future generations," Sophie replied in wonder.

"And it's also amazing that we had help from a stranger who happens to be our uncle," Scottie added. "Isn't Dr. Drake, I mean, Uncle Rusty great? I can't wait until we get to go to Auntie Jill and Rusty's wedding when we get back to our time at the ranch."

"Home . . . it seems like we've been gone for a long time."

"I know," Scottie agreed. "I miss Ma and Pa a lot. We've never been away from them for this long. I can't wait to get back to the ranch and to ride Starburst, too."

"Yes, but I'll miss Diego and our new friends from this magical place. Diego is very loyal to Dr. Drake, and he was so brave when we were on the trails and in the cave. He and Dr. Drake, I mean Uncle Rusty, have become very good friends," Sophie observed. "Anyway, let's get out of this tent so we can pack up and figure out how to get back to the ranch." Sophie was suddenly full of energy as she hopped out of her sleeping bag. She poked her head out of the now unzipped tent.

"Oh, wow, Sis, you've got to see this!"

Scottie hurried out of her sleeping bag and poked her head out of the tent too. She could hardly believe what was out there. Everywhere both girls looked, beautiful monarch butterflies were floating and feeding. They were resting on milkweed plants, trees, flowers, and even landing on Scottie's head and Sophie's shoulder!

The bright sun made their wings shimmer, just like the water in the canyon's lake.

"Why, good morning, sleepy heads," Dr. Drake announced with a smile as he walked toward them and gave both girls big hugs. "Diego set out some breakfast, so let's eat. I'm starved."

Diego was sitting on a large boulder eating a tortilla and talking with Jinx and Tomas.

"Buenos días, chicas," Diego greeted the girls.

"Good morning, Diego," they both replied with a smile.

"It's so beautiful here with the butterflies," Sophie observed.

"Yes, and without your help, we might have lost them to Professor Zooger," Tomas added as he sat on the large tree limb above their heads.

The girls beamed with pride as they sat next to Diego. Jinx walked up to the girls, knowing that they'd pet him behind his soft ears and furry neck. I sure will miss these two, he thought to himself, purring loudly.

"It's a relief to know that the monarchs are safe and can continue with their lifecycle here and throughout the world," Dr. Drake said as he ate another handful of trail mix. "And I must say, job well done, girls, job well done!"

"I agree," Diego nodded, "but I'm angry that we didn't catch Professor Zooger."

"Me, too, but now we know that he is trying to control the earth in some way in order to make money," Sophie added.

"Yes, I won't be surprised if Professor Zooger's and my path cross again in some other place and time," Dr. Drake said out loud to himself. "Well, girls, we'd better pack up. I'm sure your horses are wondering why you haven't checked up on them yet," Uncle Rusty said with a wink as he began to walk toward their tent.

The girls looked at each other in surprise and mouthed to each other, how did he know?

Sophie then ran over to help him take down the tent. "Thanks so much for all you've done for us, Dr. Drake. Actually, Scottie and I would like to call you Uncle Rusty if that's okay."

"I would love that," he replied smiling.

After Sophie helped by taking their things out of the tent, she walked over to where Tomas was perched.

"Tomas," she began, "I'd like to thank you for allowing me to be in charge of Maptrixter as well as believing in me to get everyone here to the Crystal Canyon."

"I had the utmost confidence in your abilities, my dear. And I have a feeling that you should keep the map for a while until I ask for it back," Tomas replied.

"You mean we can visit here again?" Sophie asked with excitement.

"Why, of course, we wouldn't have it any other way," Tomas told her with a twinkle in his eye.

"Icompletelyagree," Chewy said in his speed-talk as he swung down from the banyan tree.

"Oh, I didn't see you," she blurted out as she rushed over to hug him. Scottie walked over to him, too.

"You gecko monkeys are the best!" Scottie announced. "Chewy, you and your clan saved us from that awful Professor Zooger. Sophie and I will always be grateful."

"You've got that right, Sis."

"Did I hear you say, Tomas, that we can come back and visit again one day?"

"Yes, Scottie, that would be delightful," Tomas answered.

"That's awesome! Oh, it looks like Diego is about to pack up breakfast, so I'd better get some more before he does." Scottie skipped over to the food, not realizing how hungry she really was until the food was almost gone. As she ate, Scottie instinctively reached in her pocket to play with the coin she found in the rain box. She felt everywhere, but no coin. Darn, she thought, I guess I lost it. She then suddenly realized something.

"Oh, no!" Scottie exclaimed.

"What's wrong?" Sophie asked as she ran over to her.

"We forgot the rain boxes. They were such a great gift from Auntie Jill."

"I know, but remember how big they got? I don't think we could've fit them in our packs to bring them back," Sophie replied, trying to make Scottie feel better.

"Did someone mention rain boxes?" Diego asked as he walked up to give each girl her own box. "I noticed them on the ground when we were leaving. They'd shrunk to their small size again so I picked them up and threw them into my backpack."

"Oh, thank you, Diego," both girls blurted out.

"You're the best!" Scottie continued to say. Then both girls walked up to him and gave Diego a hug.

"Ah, it was nothing," Diego replied while blushing.

"I would like to give my new nieces another hug, too. You both were great on this adventure. You kept focused and never complained while we were trying to solve the monarch mystery.

"Hip, hip, hooray!" Jinx, Tomas, and Chewy cheered in agreement. Paco and Poncho dashed and darted around the girls in agreement, and Papaya squawked so loud that everyone stopped and laughed.

"Now, go finish packing," Dr. Drake ordered with a smile.

As the girls finished packing, Sophie made sure that Maptrixter was secure in her backpack. After packing, the girls walked back to everyone to say their goodbyes. Scottie got misty-eyed and Sophie's tears flowed down her cheek.

Diego suggested that he stay in the Crystal Canyon for a while to make sure all the creatures remained safe. "Since I wasn't able to capture Professor Zooger, I want to make sure that he doesn't stumble into the canyon."

"That's a great idea, Diego. We can meet back at Rancho de La Joya," Dr. Drake agreed.

Diego, Tomas, Jinx, Chewy, and the hummers escorted Sophie, Scottie, and Dr. Drake with Papaya on his shoulder to the opening of the glistening tunnel.

"What's that sound?" Sophie asked Scottie.

"I don't know, but I think it's coming from my outer pocket of my backpack," Scottie answered as she began to look in the pocket. She started to pull a few items out of her pack and then announced, "I think it's my rain box." She took it out and shook it. Sure enough, it made quite a rattling noise. Sophie walked over to see what was in it.

"Oh, how weird!" Scottie took not one, but two quarters from the box. "I guess there is one for you and one for me," Scottie discovered as she handed the quarter to Sophie.

"The quarter has the year we were born on it," the girls said to each other at the same time (as twins often do).

Suddenly, the girls felt a fierce wind as if they were lifted off the ground and then back onto the ground, like jumping from one giant boulder to another. As quickly as it started, the jumping stopped. There they stood, their feet not moving an inch.

"What just happened?" Scottie blurted out as they both turned to each other, arm in arm to steady one another from falling over.

The sound of water was behind them. Scottie and Sophie quickly turned around to see the beautiful fountain of the hotel in Rancho de La Joya! They looked at the fountain and then back to each other, not saying a word.

A few minutes passed and Sophie said, "Now I know why Uncle Rusty wanted to hug us again."

Scottie heard something and quickly turned around to look at the road near the hotel. A horse and rider were galloping near them and then on past the hotel. Both girls were hoping it would be Uncle Rusty.

"I guess that was our final goodbye from all of them," Scottie said sadly. She then looked up and across the road. "Look, Sophie!"

Across the road the girls could see a large glittering butterfly floating toward a large fir tree and moss-covered boulder. They ran across the road toward the butterfly. It seemed to disappear, but quickly the girls found out why. It floated into their bedroom! They looked at each other with excitement and began to run toward their room, jumping over small bushes and rocks.

Just when they were about to step into the room, the girls suddenly stopped. Each turned around to get a glimpse of this beautiful land, the fountain, and the hotel, where this amazing adventure began. Scottie and Sophie then looked at each other, hooked arms, and walked into their room with their packs still on their backs. The butterfly floated around their heads and then flew out into the trees.

"Goodbye, Bella," the girls said while waving.

Instantly, the frame shrunk back to its original size, glowing on the bedroom floor in many colors of yellow, green, blue, and orange. Scottie picked it up off the floor and put the frame on the table. The girls took their backpacks off and just stared at the picture. Suddenly, the picture began to glow and faded away. Sophie gasped and reached for the frame to take the picture out, but it was too late. The frame was blank.

With a sigh, Sophie said, "Why did that have to happen? Now how do we ever get back?"

"I don't know. We just have to trust that Auntie Jill will send us another picture so we can visit the Crystal Canyon one day," Scottie replied in a sad voice.

"We'd better put this table back. Look, the window is still open," Sophie pointed as Scottie walked over to close it.

"I don't know about you, but let's go find Ma and Pa!" She then began to run toward the door.

Just as the girls ran into the living room, they could see Ma and Pa talking to a man in a chair with his back to them.

"Oh, here are my girls, and in such a hurry I see," Ma said in amusement as they ran up to hug her.

"We have a guest," Pa said as the man stood up to turn toward them.

Both girls gasped and instantly looked at each other and looked at the man.

"This is Dr. Drake," Pa introduced to them. "Dr. Drake, these are our two daughters, Sophie and Scottie."

The girls walked toward him in shock as he took their hands and shook them.

"It's so nice to meet you two. I've heard a lot about you from your Aunt Jill," he said with a wink. "Oh, and by the way," Dr. Drake continued with a smile. "I have an envelope from your aunt to give to you."

Sophie and Scottie, still stunned, didn't move.

"Well, is anyone going to take the envelope?" Pa asked.

They reached for the envelope and looked at each other and then at Dr. Drake.

"I think it's a photograph!" Sophie exclaimed breathlessly to Scottie.

Scottie took the envelope, opened it, and looked inside. She looked up at Dr. Drake and then to Sophie and said excitedly, "I think you're right!"

TO BE CONTINUED…

ABOUT THE AUTHOR

Cindy C. Murray

Cindy C. Murray loves sharing engaging and imaginative stories with young readers. Her creative storytelling is inspired by her two daughters and by the childhood adventures she shared with her six siblings. She has received a Bachelor of Science degree in Business Administration as well as several book awards; Silver Mom's Choice Award, Gold Family Choice Award, and Silver International Readers' Favorite. She lives in Rowlett, Texas, with her husband, visiting daughters, and two dogs.

www.cindycmurray.com

Sophie and Scottie's Adventures
of Something's Fishy

Both girls looked at their magical frame that Auntie Jill had given them. It still looked the same as it did before their adventure to Mexico with hundreds of tiny mirrored crystals covering it and a large diamond shaped crystal in the middle of the top of the frame.

"The frame seems so normal," Scottie commented as she looked at it displayed on their round oak table in the 'safe' zone of their bedroom, "it isn't glowing or changing colors, or getting larger. No, it just looks normal."

Just as Scottie said that, the frame suddenly slid across the table next to the envelope! And then the frame seemed to come alive with colors of soft yellow, then bright yellow; then soft orange, changing into bright orange. Then, as if with a sigh, the frame went from bright blue to sky blue and then back to its beautiful clear and silver crystals.

It seemed like days since the twin sisters had been back on the ranch. Sophie and Scottie had learned so much about team work and trust, but will they be ready for the next adventure the new photograph and the magical frame has in store for them? As they follow Auntie Jill's directions and finally look at the picture, is it really of an island in the Pacific Ocean?

Come and join the sisters on their magical adventure in:

Sophie and Scottie's Adventures of Something's Fishy!

Sophie and Scottie's Adventures
of Sweet Tooth Rock

Sophie and Scottie were happy when they returned from Amelia Island to Shear Heaven Ranch on horseback. Their "fishy" adventure was amazing, full of action, new friends, and a bit of magic! But now the sisters were ready to stay home and enjoy their summer for a while. Little did they know that events were about to happen on the ranch that were out of their control!

Oh no, it was a storm like no other and the girls had to help Pa save their birthing ewe, Fuzzy Mama, as well as the barn from flooding. Luckily, the storm passed after Scottie had to drive the tractor and Sophie recovered after falling off her horse during their first annual rodeo to help raise funds for the storm damaged school gym.

With all of the comotion, Pa forgot to give Sophie and Scottie an envelope from their Auntie Jill! Was it another picture to activate their magical frame? What adventure will be ahead of them if it is? Find out the answers to these questions and more when you join the girls in their next action packed journey:

Sophie and Scottie's Adventures
of Sweet Tooth Rock!

CPSIA information can be obtained
at www.ICGtesting.com
Printed in the USA
FFHW010422250119
50262669-55266FF